obert Rigby is the author of *The Eagle Trail*, as well as the co-author, with Andy McNab, of the best-ng *Boy Soldier* series. His other fiction includes the lizations of the *Goal!* movies and a stand-alone novel e series, *Goal: Glory Days*. He is the author of the four cial London 2012 Olympic and Paralympic novels for lren. Robert also writes for theatre, television and o, and is a prolific songwriter and composer. He lives xford.

ou can visit Robert at **www.robertrigby.co.uk**

CODENAME

THE ENEMY HAS LANDED

EAGLE

ROBERT RIGBY

WALKER
BOOKS

First published 2015 by Walker Books Ltd
87 Vauxhall Walk, London SE11 5HJ

This edition published 2015

2 4 6 8 10 9 7 5 3 1

Text © 2015 Robert Rigby
Cover image of young man © Getty Images, Inc
Cover images of paratroopers and men in uniform
© 2015 Sergey Kamshylin / Shutterstock.com

This book has been typeset in M Times New Roman

Printed and bound in Great Britain by Clays Ltd, St Ives plc

British Library Cataloguing in Publication Data:
a catalogue record for this book is available from the British Library

ISBN 978-1-4063-4667-1

www.walker.co.uk

To Reynard

PROLOGUE

South-west France, autumn 1940

Gaston Rouzard was in a foul temper. He had drunk far too much cheap red wine the previous evening and fallen into a troubled sleep in a lumpy armchair.

Soon after dawn he was roughly shaken awake by his grinning, unsympathetic friend, Raymond Martel, and without breakfast or even his usual cup of strong black coffee, he hurried to Chalabre station to catch the first train to Lavelanet, where he lived and worked as a gendarme, and where he was due to go on duty.

When Gaston bustled, panting and sweating, into the gendarmerie, the phone was ringing. He flinched as the sound clanged in his thudding head, then picked up the receiver and barked into the mouthpiece: "Yes, what is it?"

In a few urgent words the caller explained the situation. An explosive device had been detonated beneath a railway bridge on an isolated stretch of track between Lavelanet and Foix. Part of the bridge was down and the track was blocked; trains could not pass. It was chaos, and it needed sorting.

"Who is this?" Gaston growled.

"Look, it's dangerous there; I have to get back. And you'd better come quick," the caller replied before hanging up.

The call did not improve Gaston's temper. "More trouble," he moaned, walking out of the gendarmerie. "So many troublemakers, and always me who has to sort them out."

Gaston had never learned to drive, so he ignored the Citroën in the police yard and went to the motorized bicycle resting against one wall.

He hated riding the thing: he was too big for it and he felt stupid when the people of Lavelanet saw him chugging slowly through the streets. But he had no option; he was alone on duty so there was no one else to go to the incident.

He mounted the bicycle, pushed the small motor into position against the front wheel and pedalled away. The two-stroke engine coughed into life.

Gaston felt as grubby as he looked – and, he realized, smelled. He was unwashed and unshaven, alcohol seemed to be oozing from every pore in his body, there was a sour, bitter taste in his mouth and he still hadn't had the cup of strong coffee he craved.

Fortunately, the scene of the incident wasn't too far out of town, and soon he was turning off the main road onto what was little more than a farm track with wide fields on either side.

The bicycle bounced over dried mud and deep ruts, and Gaston's mood darkened with each bump and shudder. He couldn't afford to be away from Lavelanet this morning. He needed to know about last night's mission. Had it been as successful as he anticipated? If all had gone to plan, it meant success for him and not for his enemies.

"I hope they got everything they deserve," he grunted, smiling for the first time that day.

There were no houses or farm buildings on the narrow track, just the occasional stand of wind-bent trees and clump of scrubby bush. After five minutes of bumping along in a slow curve, there was a sudden, hard right turn where the road met the railway line and ran alongside it as the ground sloped sharply downwards.

The damaged bridge was less than a mile ahead. Gaston knew the spot; he'd passed beneath the bridge many times on train journeys. It went under another small road used mainly by farm vehicles and carts.

"Why do they do it?" Gaston said aloud, his temper rising again. "Kids. I'll bet it was kids – some pathetic gesture over the war. But the war has nothing to do with us any more. We're out of it."

He pulled the bicycle to a standstill at a place where a rusted metal water trough blocked the way, marking the end of the road. Gaston would have to walk the last hundred metres or so.

Easing himself off the saddle, he wearily rested the machine against the trough and was suddenly chilled by the stiff breeze sweeping down from the Pyrenees. He glanced up towards the towering peaks and wondered again about the mission that had taken place last night. He would hear the news soon enough.

Gaston shivered and then blinked in the bright daylight, still groggy from the session of heavy drinking. Reaching down, he dipped the fingers of one hand into the murky water in the trough. It was icy. Winter was coming.

He ran two wet fingers across his aching brow, flinched, then trudged forward, pushing aside thin, straggling branches as the track narrowed to a footpath.

"Hello!" he called, glimpsing the bridge through the bushes and overhanging branches. "I'm here! Gaston Rouzard! Gendarme! Where are you?"

There was no answer. The only sound was the distant cawing of crows.

"Bloody typical," Gaston said, pushing on. "They call me to sort things out and then leave me to it. How am I supposed to repair a bridge? I'm a policeman, not a bloody railway engineer."

The bridge sat in a clearing, and as Gaston nudged aside the last branch blocking his view, his eyes widened and he stopped walking. There was no sign of any damage. No fallen bricks or stone, no rubble of any description on the track.

"What the…? What's going on here?"

Warily, he stepped over the closest rail and on to the track, his boots crunching on the ballast bed and tarred wooden sleepers as he got closer to the bridge. "Must be on the other side," he muttered.

He walked under the single arch into shadow and gloom. The bricks above his head were damp and mossy, but none had fallen onto the track. It looked perfectly clear in both directions.

Gaston sighed angrily as he moved back into the light. "It's a bloody joke," he snarled. "Someone's got me out here on a wild goose chase!"

"No, Gaston," a voice behind him said. "It's not a joke."

Gaston spun around and then stared. "You! What are you doing here?"

The man facing him didn't reply.

"Look," Gaston snapped, "I don't have time for playing games. You of all people should know that."

"It's no game, Gaston."

"Then what's going on? Why here? We could have met in town."

"No. Not this time."

"What are you talking about?" The anger in Gaston's eyes changed to a look of concern. "Last night," he said quickly. "Did something go wrong last night?"

"Oh, yes, something went wrong. Something went *very* wrong. They found out about Yvette Bigou."

"Yvette? But how – how could they?"

"Because she failed the one task she was given. So I dealt with her before they could get to her."

"Dealt with her? I don't…"

Gaston fell silent as he watched the man pull a snub-nosed pistol from the right pocket of his jacket.

"And now, Gaston, I have to deal with you. You're too much of a liability."

"No. No, wait," Gaston gasped. "No, that's impossible. You can't shoot me, not you… I'm taking over … me…"

His trembling hands snatched at the holster on his belt, fingers fumbling desperately at the flap covering his police issue handgun.

But it was already too late. The pistol spat out a round. Gaston heard the sound just as the bullet punched into his chest and sent him sprawling to the ground beside the track.

He lay there, terrified and bewildered, his face in the dirt. There was a roaring in his ears, tears in his eyes and a sudden sweet taste in his mouth. He so desperately needed that cup of coffee to wash away the sweet taste in his mouth.

He heard footsteps and the pistol sounded again.

And then Gaston knew no more.

ONE

April 1941. Day One.

Paul Hansen stared moodily at the flickering flames in the wood-burning stove; its double-hinged doors were wide open for maximum heat.

The steady ticking of the slate clock invaded Paul's thoughts and he glanced across at it; why did clocks always tick more loudly when you were waiting for something to happen? It was almost time for the BBC news bulletin from London. Listening to BBC broadcasts was illegal in France, even in the Free Zone. But those who wanted to know about the progress of the war took the risk and listened anyway. And Paul Hansen had an almost obsessive need to know about the progress of the war.

It had been a long and bone-achingly cold winter. Paul could scarcely believe that the sun-drenched south-west France, which he'd first encountered at the end of the previous summer, could turn so bitingly cold in wintertime. Growing up in England and Belgium, he had never experienced such cold. There had been frosty days, ice and occasionally thick snow, of course, but nothing remotely like the winter that had just ended. On some days, with smoke from the stoves in every home in Lavelanet climbing into low grey cloud, the temperature had plummeted to minus 19 or 20 degrees.

And throughout those hard months, each time Paul gazed towards the snow-topped peaks of the Pyrenees, he was reminded of his failed attempt to cross those mountains into Spain, and of the brutal deaths that marked that failure. The memory was always with him, like so many other memories of the past months.

But at last spring was arriving. Heavy rains were washing away the snow from the lower slopes, swelling the rivers; trees were putting on new leaves and the ground was warming. Most nights were still bitterly cold though, and tonight was no exception.

Paul felt restless and unsettled. He turned to his friend Didier Brunet, who was sitting, equally thoughtful, in a second chair facing the stove.

"Time for the news," Paul said.

Didier got up and went to the radio set perched on a cupboard. He switched it on and the dull yellow light illuminating the dial grew brighter as the valve warmed. The set was never left tuned to London; it was wise to be careful, even in the Free Zone.

The radio whined and whistled as Didier turned the dial; fragments of French and German came through fleetingly before the familiar chimes of Big Ben sounded. Didier settled back into his chair as the newsreader began to speak.

The news was not good. The Germans' blitz of London and other major cities was continuing. There had been air raids on Portsmouth, Plymouth and Bristol, and in Scotland, the Luftwaffe had bombed Glasgow and the shipping area along the River Clyde. Fighting between German and British troops in Africa was intensifying and, reading between the lines, it appeared that the enemy was gaining the upper hand. And in the Atlantic, German U-boats had struck again at merchant shipping, inflicting heavy losses.

Paul spoke English as well as he spoke French, but Didier understood only the words and phrases he had picked up from his friend and the BBC, so as the broadcast continued, he frequently asked Paul to translate.

When the bulletin was over and the set switched off, they lapsed into a gloomy silence, with Paul's mood darkening even more. He had recently turned seventeen, but the events of the previous seven or eight months had forced him to grow up quickly. He picked out a log from the wicker basket and tossed it into the open stove. Sparks hissed and crackled, and burning ashes spat onto the wooden floorboards.

"Sorry," Paul said quickly, jumping to his feet and stamping on the smouldering embers.

Didier smiled. "I know the news is bad, but there's no need to burn the house down; my mother wouldn't be pleased."

Paul forced a smile and sank down onto his chair. "I feel

useless, Didier. The war gets worse by the day and we sit here doing nothing."

"All we can do is wait," Didier said.

"It's not as though I'm meant to be here, anyway," Paul continued, as though not hearing Didier's words. "I should have been in England long before now. I could have joined the army and been out there fighting somewhere."

"I doubt it," Didier said. He was a year and a half older than his friend, and more patient by nature. "You're not actually old enough to join the army."

"I'll lie about my age. I wouldn't be the first."

"Last year you said you wanted to stay here to continue the fight. Remember?"

"Of course I remember, but it's been six months and we haven't fought anyone. We haven't done a thing. I thought we'd at least get Gaston Rouzard, but someone even beat us to that."

"To keep him quiet," Didier said. "And that means whoever killed Gaston is still around. Biding his time. Listen, it's like Henri says, it's difficult to be an effective resistance group when there are no Germans here to fight."

Didier was right. France, along with Belgium and the Netherlands, had surrendered to Germany in June of the previous year. Since then, the northern part of the country and the whole Atlantic coast had been occupied by the Germans, while the southern Free Zone was officially out of the war and being governed by a hastily organized French administration based in the town of Vichy.

But few were fooled. The Germans held southern France in an iron grip: even though they were not actually present, their spies, informers and collaborators certainly were.

"I don't think I can wait any longer," said Paul in response to Didier's earlier words.

"What do you mean?"

"If the Germans won't come to us, then I'll have to go to them."

"And how do you intend to do that?"

"Spain first, and then England and the army. The weather's improving, I'll ask Henri if I can make another attempt to get across the mountains into Spain. Just because the guides turned out to be murderers and thieves last time doesn't mean we can't find others to do the job."

"Yes," Didier said nodding, "there are plenty of true patriots who will take you across. So you've changed your mind – you do want to leave after all?"

Paul hesitated. "Look, Didier, you've all been so good to me; I feel at home here. And I don't have any other home now, not since..."

Didier knew what his friend had been about to say. "I can understand you hating the Germans, Paul, after what they did to your parents. And I can understand you wanting your revenge."

"But it's not just about revenge, and I don't hate all Germans. There are good and bad Germans."

"And good and bad French and good and bad English," Didier said, smiling.

Paul nodded. "It's the Nazis and everything they stand for that I hate. And in one way I admire the Germans."

"Really?" Didier asked, raising his eyebrows. "In what way, exactly?"

"They're ruthless. And if we want to win this war we have to be ruthless too. I want to part of it."

"Our chance will come, Paul. Be patient for a little longer."

"I can't," Paul said, shaking his head. "My mind's made up, I'm going to speak to Henri."

"And what about Josette?"

The burning wood crackled and spat, and the flames from the stove cast flickering shadows on the walls of the small sitting room.

"Yes," Paul said, looking into the flames. "What about Josette?"

TWO

They came in the night like phantoms, dropping noiselessly from a starlit sky, and landed soft as shadows on the frosty grassland.

And as the six silent men began gathering in the billowing material that trailed behind them, a seventh parachute floated down, the steel container suspended beneath it thudding more heavily onto the ground.

High above, a Junkers Ju-52 was circling, turning northwards, the steady drone of its engines already getting fainter.

The parachutists had landed in an area covering no more than 600 metres, following a single narrow beam of light that had guided the aircraft to the drop zone. The beam continued to shine as two of the men collected the chutes and followed their leader towards the light source.

The three others hurried to the container. One took responsibility for the parachute while the others disconnected the steel cylinder and picked it up, one at each end. Then all three followed the others towards the light.

Since the landing, not a single word had been spoken by

any of the six men. They all knew exactly what to do. They were dressed in paratrooper jumpsuits, but were members of the Brandenburg Regiment, a German army Special Forces unit specializing in commando-type covert operations behind enemy lines.

The regiment was made up mainly of Germans who had lived abroad and were fluent in other languages. All six of these men could speak French, and the officer in charge spoke English too.

Aside from their ability with languages, they were elite soldiers: experts in fighting with small arms and in unarmed combat, and highly skilled in demolition and sabotage.

As they approached, a middle-aged Frenchman switched off the powerful torch, and the silhouette of a heavy lorry with a canvas covered back became visible to the soldiers.

The German officer wasted no time with introductions. "I'll ride in the cab with you," he said in perfect French to the waiting man. "The others will go in the back."

The Frenchman, short and stocky, with a bright red face and a bulging beer gut, watched in silence as the soldiers swiftly and efficiently lifted the steel container into the back of the lorry and climbed in.

Then the Frenchman and the German officer got into the cab, the engine rumbled into life and the lorry moved off across the flat expanse of the Plateau de Sault in the direction of the small town of Bélesta.

In the back, the Brandenburgers were working quickly.

First they removed their jumpsuits. Beneath them, two wore the uniforms of French gendarmes; the others were dressed like farm workers.

In the cab, the officer was also removing his jumpsuit, to reveal another gendarme uniform.

The driver smiled, nodding his approval. "Very convincing."

"Of course it's convincing," the officer said quickly. "It's genuine. You have our car ready?"

"It's in a barn, back at the wood yard. Along with my own vehicle."

"And this lorry?"

"It belongs to my two friends at the yard."

"You're certain they can be trusted?"

"Oh, yes. They're simple lads, but trustworthy; they'll do exactly as they're told and keep their mouths shut. Times are hard, so for them it's a chance to make a little extra. It's different for me, of course, a matter of principle, and I'm honoured to meet you."

The officer ignored the ingratiating comment. "Tell me about the car."

The Frenchman grinned. "It was easy enough to arrange, through a friend in Toulouse. You'd think the police would look after their vehicles more carefully, wouldn't you? The fuel to run it is another matter; not so easy to come by since rationing."

"But you're being paid to make sure we have fuel, and

anything else we need, come to that."

"Don't get me wrong, I'm not complaining," the Frenchman said quickly. He smiled again and wiped the back of one hand across his stubby, bent nose. "I'm very happy with the financial arrangements, and I have a contact who gets me fuel. He can get almost anything."

"Then you are fortunate."

"But for me it's not just the money. I'm doing it for the cause. For us."

The officer slowly turned his head to stare at the driver. "Us?"

"Yes, us," the driver said, nodding his head vigorously. "I may be French, but I'm a Nazi like you, and I believe in the same things as you do."

"Oh, do you?"

"Yes, most certainly. *Heil Hitler*!"

As he spoke, the Frenchman lifted his right hand from the steering wheel and attempted a German salute, but the flat glass windscreen prevented him from fully extending his arm, making the gesture look ridiculous.

The officer made no attempt to disguise his contempt. "To many of your countrymen you'd be considered a traitor. In the north they are already sending tiny wooden coffins marked with a cross to suspected collaborators."

If the Frenchman was perturbed by the German's comment he didn't let it show. "I've heard of that. Wooden coffins or little drawings; like kids'. They're misguided fools. They'll learn in time."

"You think so? Well, let me make this clear: I'm German, but I am *not* a Nazi. I'm a soldier doing my duty for my country, and that's all."

"I understand, of course, but—"

"Then understand this," the officer interrupted, giving the Frenchman no option but to hold his tongue. "I'll work with you because, unfortunately, we need people like you." He paused, then his voice hardened. "But don't ever describe you and me as *us*."

The Frenchman said nothing more.

The vehicle had moved off the plateau and was on the stretch of road dropping down through the forest of Bélesta. After ten minutes the driver turned off onto a mud track, which meandered for more than a kilometre through rows of giant silver fir trees. The dim headlights picked out stacks of cut logs dotted along the fringes of the track and then illuminated a large wood-built house.

There was a sudden, quick movement in the darkness, and the headlights briefly lit up the black eyes of a snarling dog, tethered on a long chain.

"The barn's at the back," the Frenchman said, ignoring the dog and driving past the house into a wide yard with a barn at the far side.

Two men stood waiting by the back door of the house.

"Pull up here," the officer ordered. "We'll unload our equipment and then I'll take a look at the car."

The driver brought the lorry to a standstill, got out and went to the waiting men, who were in their mid-twenties. They stood watching while the German soldiers swiftly carried clothes, light weapons, a radio transmitter and other equipment into the farmhouse – and even cartons of cigarettes and slabs of wrapped chocolate.

The dog was still barking angrily.

"Can't you shut that thing up?" the German officer said to one of the younger men.

"No need; there's no one to hear. And he'll stop barking when he gets fed up."

The officer nodded and was about to go into the house when he stopped and studied the two young Frenchmen standing side by side. It was like seeing double. They were twins, big and strong-looking, and even in the dull yellow light spilling from one window and the open door it was obvious that they were identical. The officer made no comment; he simply looked from one face to the other before nodding again and going inside.

"He's a miserable sod," the lorry driver said quietly to the twins. "And ungrateful. No appreciation of what we're doing for him, or of the risks we're taking."

The twins exchanged a look, apparently sharing the same thought. "Doesn't worry Eddie and me, we're only in it for the money," one of them said. "And so as long as they keep paying, they can be as miserable as they like. When do we get the final payment?"

"The big payment," his brother added with a grin.

"When it's all over," the older man said. "Before they leave." He glanced through the window into the house. "They're a tough lot, though, these Brandenburgers. They say every one of them carries a suicide pill in case he's captured behind enemy lines."

"They're not behind enemy lines," the twin called Eddie said. "We're not at war with anyone in the Free Zone."

"But they can't just drop in on us," the older man insisted, "not according to the new laws. This must be important, and I'd like to know why."

"So ask them."

"Maybe I will."

Eddie smiled. "Come on inside, we'll make coffee."

Fifteen minutes later, the three Frenchman and six Germans sat on a variety of unmatched chairs and benches around a huge, scrubbed wooden table, drinking coffee and smoking cigarettes. Old oil lamps, belching as much smoke as flame, made the air dense and fuggy.

Outside, the dog continued to bark.

The German officer looked at one of the twins. "You said that animal would stop barking."

The twin smiled. "It was my brother, Gilbert, who told you that. I'm Eddie, the good-looking one, and the younger one."

"By ten minutes," Gilbert chipped in.

"And the fact is," Eddie continued, "the dog always barks

when there are strangers around. That's what he's here for. But don't worry, he's on a chain."

"A long chain," Gilbert said.

The German officer ignored the attempt to lighten the mood as he looked from one twin to the other. They really were identical. Above average height, broad-shouldered and muscular, with dark, curly hair and square faces.

"You live alone here?" the officer asked.

"Just us and our barking dog," Eddie said, still smiling.

"And the horse," his brother added.

"Oh, yes," Eddie said. "And the horse. He helps us shift the logs."

"And he's a lot more use to me than you are," the older twin laughed, thumping his younger brother on the arm.

"Look, can we get on?" the man who had driven the lorry said impatiently. "I must get back to Lavelanet. I have to work in the morning and I start early."

"We'll go over the details and you can leave," the officer told him. "Is the target still at the address you've given us?"

The Frenchman nodded. "He's been living there for six months or more."

"And there's no indication that he suspects he's being watched?"

"None. I've been careful."

"I'll take a look tomorrow."

"You want me to show you the way?"

The officer shook his head. "We have maps of the town

and the area." He turned to the twins. "But I'd like one of you to go back to the plateau with two of my men. They need to fix the best place for our plane to land for the pick-up."

"Don't bother with that," the older Frenchman said. "The best place is exactly where you landed. That's why I chose it."

"We'll make sure of that for ourselves," the officer said. "In daylight. And we'll take the target the day after tomorrow, early morning." He stood up. "So unless you are unclear on anything, my men and I would like to get some rest."

The Frenchman took a long drag at his cigarette and then stubbed it out. "There is one thing."

"Yes?"

"Why all this urgency? Why not let the real gendarmes arrest him? He'd be in your hands soon enough, anyway. They'd hold him here for a while and then shift him up to the Occupied Zone, or even to Germany. Not that the twins and I are complaining, of course; we're happy to do our bit."

"Yes, I can see that," the German replied. "And as far as your question is concerned, all you need to know is that he's important to us – extremely important. And we want him. Now. Does that satisfy you?"

"Oh, perfectly, sir," the Frenchman said, his smile of earlier returning. "Perfectly."

THREE
Day Two

Josette Mazet did not look happy. Her dark eyes were narrowed and her lips were clamped tight. She was fighting to stop herself from flying into one of her famous rages and was just about managing to keep her mouth shut. Just about.

Her father, Henri, sat behind his desk, one finger rhythmically stroking his bushy moustache as he considered what Paul had just told him.

Paul looked at Henri, waiting for his response, while Didier leaned against the closed door. It was important that no one outside the office heard what was being discussed, even though the thunderous noise from the looms down on the factory floor would make any words spoken in the room inaudible to anyone in the corridor. But it was best and safest to be certain.

Henri sighed and then nodded to Paul. "Of course, I'll start making enquiries. It may take a little while, but I'm sure we can get you across the mountains before too long. And we'll be sure to make a better job of it this time."

"Thank you, Henri," Paul said. "You know how much I

appreciate everything you've done for me."

Josette could no longer stay silent. "Oh, that's kind of you," she said angrily. "Why didn't you say something before? Or even last night when you got back from Didier's?"

Paul had lived with Henri Mazet and his family since arriving in Lavelanet the previous year. "It was late," he said. "And … and I didn't want to upset your mother."

"My mother! What about Papa? What about me?"

"Well, all of you. I knew it would come as a bit of a shock."

"Oh, you're right about that, it is a shock! So is that why you were too cowardly to come out and tell us before now? Is that it?"

"Josette!" Henri said.

"No, Papa," Josette continued furiously. "It is cowardly of him to say nothing until the very last minute."

Paul took a deep breath, forcing himself to stay calm and not be drawn into an argument with Josette. He was far from a coward. Twice in the previous year he had fought bravely, for his own life and for the lives of his friends. But when Josette was in one of her rages his bravery somehow seemed to disappear. "I'm sorry, Josette," he said quietly, "but I wasn't sure myself until a couple of days ago. And you're right; I should have told you then. But I've told you now, and I'll say it once more so there's no doubt in anyone's mind: I do want to leave Lavelanet and try to get to England. And I'm…"

"Oh, well, thank you for letting us know! At last!" Josette snarled, unwilling to listen to any further words of explanation. "And you will be sure to let us know when you change your mind again, won't you!"

She sprang up from her chair, sending it crashing to the floor as she marched quickly towards the door.

Didier was in her way. He considered saying something, but when he saw her furious glare, swiftly changed his mind and stepped aside. Josette wrenched open the door and stormed out, slamming it so hard that the glass in the office windows shuddered.

Paul looked at Henri, who shrugged and gave him a slight smile. "She'll be all right when she calms down."

"I'll go after her," Didier said, picking up the chair and setting it by Josette's desk. "You don't need me here."

He winked reassuringly at Paul and left the room, closing the door much more quietly than Josette had.

Henri stared at the young man facing him. He had changed in the past few months, grown up – perhaps too quickly, but that was hardly surprising after what he'd been through. He'd become more confident, assertive and, it now appeared, decisive. "Now, Paul, are you quite certain about your decision?"

"Yes, Henri," Paul replied without hesitation. "I'm absolutely certain." He felt himself relaxing; the tension that had been building suddenly eased now that he had finally admitted to himself and everyone else that he wanted and needed to leave Lavelanet. The long, hard winter and the surrounding mountains had somehow combined to make him feel trapped, hemmed in. Now that would change, but so would the relationships he had built with all those he had grown so close to over the past months – particularly Josette.

Paul was getting used to change, and yet before the war and despite his complicated family background – he was part English, part French and part Belgian – his life had been so simple. His father had been an important civil engineer, specializing in the modernization and rebuilding of all the largest harbours and docks in Europe, including those in Germany.

And while Edward Hansen and his wife, Clarisse, crisscrossed Europe, Paul attended an English boarding school until the age of fourteen. Then, when his parents eventually settled in Antwerp, Belgium, Paul joined them.

Even when war came, with the Germans occupying the whole of northern Europe, Paul had still somehow felt that it wasn't really affecting him too seriously: his life carried on largely as it had before.

But his comfortable existence was shattered in a single brutal moment when he saw his father shot and killed by German soldiers. That same day his mother was arrested and taken away by the Nazis. No word had been heard of her since.

The following day, Paul had begun his journey across Belgium and down through France for the attempt to escape to freedom across the Pyrenees. Only then did he learn that his father had not only been leading the Resistance movement in Antwerp, he had also operated as a spy for the Allies, making detailed plans of the German harbours and their defences.

And although Edward Hansen had been dead for more than six months, the plans he had made were still in existence. Somewhere.

Paul was deep in thought, reliving his escape from Belgium, thinking about his mother and father and the times they had shared. Suddenly a new thought flashed into his mind as he remembered a conversation with his father about a hiding place, a perfect hiding place.

"Oh!" Paul gasped. "Of course!"

He looked across at Henri, who was staring at him. "What is it, Paul? Is there something else you want to tell me?"

Paul nodded. "Yes, there is, Henri. And I think it's important, very important. It's about my father."

FOUR

It was a bright, warm spring morning; the sun blazed proudly in a sky of deep, almost unnatural blue.

Josette sat on the café terrace staring at an untouched cup of coffee. Didier sat opposite her, waiting for the outburst, which he suspected would arrive at any moment.

He had followed Josette to the café after being informed by the factory foreman, Marcel Castelnaud, that she had thundered down the stairs and swept out of the building without a word to anyone.

"Looked to be in one of her tempers, so I didn't say anything," Marcel had told him.

Didier took a guess at where Josette might have gone to collect her thoughts, and he was right. It was a café they went to quite often, usually with Paul.

He took a seat, ordered a coffee for himself and waited. The coffee arrived; Didier took a sip, replaced the cup on the saucer and then waited some more.

"I brought him here," Josette said at last, without looking at Didier, "when he first came to Lavelanet. I hadn't been very friendly until then, so I brought him here to talk. And that was the first time I … I realized that I did like him … a bit. I shouldn't have bothered being so nice."

Didier expected Josette to continue, but she fell into a brooding silence.

"Your coffee's getting cold."

"I don't care about the coffee," Josette snapped. "I don't want it."

Didier smiled sympathetically. "It's always been a bit stormy between you two, hasn't it? And anyway, I've been telling you for months that I'm the one for you. You should have accepted that long ago." He laughed. "Look, I know you like Paul too, but face up to it, Josette, you and I were made for each other."

Despite her anger, Josette couldn't stop herself from laughing. She'd known Didier for most of her life and she liked him a lot. But when he'd spoken of his feelings for her the previous year, she'd told him she wasn't interested in a boyfriend – any boyfriend.

Her brother, Venant, had been killed fighting for his country just a few months earlier, and then all Josette had wanted was to be part of the Resistance movement, to fight back against the Germans.

But then Paul turned up and, although Josette's commitment to the war effort hadn't wavered, her thoughts about a boyfriend had. She did like Paul. And she also liked Didier, but not in quite the same way.

Didier was good-looking: tall – a little taller than Paul – and dark-haired, with a strong face and twinkling eyes. You knew where you stood with Didier; he was solid and totally reliable.

Paul was different. He was good-looking, too. In fact, Josette thought as she pictured Paul in her mind, he could actually be described as *handsome*. His fair hair and striking blue eyes made him stand out in southern France. Josette reckoned he looked a bit like one of those American film stars she'd watched at the cinema in Lavelanet. She'd never told him that, of course. The trouble with Paul, though, was that he was complicated; you were never entirely sure what he was thinking.

"Or what he's going to do next," she suddenly said aloud.

"What?" Didier asked.

"Nothing," Josette said, with a shake of her head. "Why does he want to go, Didier? What's wrong with us? He told me you're the best friend he's ever had."

"He saved my life in the mountains last year."

"And you saved his."

Didier shrugged modestly. "I suppose that gives us some kind of special bond."

"So then why does he want to leave?"

"Josette, you and I have lived here all our lives. This is our home. This is the place and these are the people we want to fight for. It's not the same for Paul. The war is a bigger picture for him, and the world is a bigger place."

"But he said he wanted to stay and help us."

"Yes, but when he arrived here things were different. When your father and me, and Gaston Rouzard and—"

"That traitor!" Josette interrupted, eyes blazing. "I would have killed him myself."

"Yes, I know, you've told me before, but just listen for once."

Josette glared at him.

"Please?" Didier said.

She took a breath and sat back in her chair.

Didier leaned closer, speaking softly. "When the four of us – your father and me, Gaston and Jean-Pierre Dilhat – set up the Resistance cell, we expected more to join us."

"But it didn't happen," Josette said, glancing towards the distant mountains. "Even though Jean-Pierre gave his life for us up there."

"No," Didier said with a shake of his head, "it hasn't worked out as we hoped."

Josette was still looking at the mountains. "My grandmother says people here have seen too much war and they're tired of it, so they don't get involved or they ignore it and pretend it's not happening." She turned back to Didier, her face angry again. "But it is happening, Didier, and we can't ignore it. And when the Germans come marching in here like they did in the north, then everyone who hasn't bothered will be sorry. Because then it'll be too late."

"Shh," Didier said softly. "Keep your voice down. It

won't be too late, and we'll be ready. It's just a pity that Paul won't be with us after all."

They were quiet for a couple of minutes, each lost in their own thoughts. Then Josette picked up her coffee cup, took a sip and grimaced. "It's cold."

"I told you it was. Shall we order some more?"

They were alone on the terrace. Josette glanced towards the café. Through the window she could see the owner, Victor Forêt, standing behind the bar. He appeared to be in a heated argument with one of his customers.

"Look at those two," Josette said to Didier. "Plenty to say as usual, and I'll bet it's about nothing important. I wouldn't exactly say I'm fighting for people like those two."

"Oh, Victor's all right."

"You think everyone's all right."

"I don't, but Victor's never done me any harm."

Before Josette could say any more, the café door flew back and a young man staggered out and crashed into one of the terrace tables. He yelled in pain, then stumbled and fell to the ground.

Victor Forêt was pursuing him. "And you can stay out! You're banned! Go and drink your beer somewhere else. You're not wanted here."

"Oh, I'll stay out," the young man said, slowly getting to his feet and rubbing his bruised leg. "But I won't forget this. And you'll be sorry for what you just did, very sorry."

"Are you threatening me?" Forêt said, clenching his fist

and taking a step towards the younger man.

"You'll see, Victor, you'll see," the young man said, backing away. He noticed Josette and Didier staring, and gave them a hostile glare before limping off the terrace and across the small square.

The café owner watched him go, both hands resting on his huge beer gut. His round, podgy face was even redder than usual. He sniffed loudly and wiped the back of one hand across his nose.

Then the scowl he wore turned to a smile as he realized Josette and Didier were watching him. "Argument over rugby got a little out of hand," he said, the smile fixed to his face. "But that Alain Noury; always boasting, spoiling for a fight." He took a deep breath and wiped his hand across his face a second time. "Now what can I get you? More coffee?"

Josette stood up. "No, thanks, we're leaving."

She dropped a few coins onto the table and she and Didier made their way from the terrace, conscious of the bar owner's eyes on them.

"Rugby!" Josette hissed between clenched teeth.

FIVE

When the sun shone and the sky was clear, the Plateau de Sault looked a benign and beautiful place.

Wide, flat grasslands and wetlands, dotted here and there with exotic wild orchids, formed a seemingly safe and secure haven for grazing cattle. At almost a thousand metres above sea level, the air was crisp and clean, and the snow-topped mountains ringing the plateau completed a picture postcard-like scene.

But the Plateau de Sault was deceptive, keeping close its treacherous secrets. Snow and ice had spent centuries eroding the limestone surface, remorselessly carving out hundreds of underground caves and deep, open surface wells.

In winter, the plateau was frequently cut off from the surrounding communities. Wind-whipped snow would pile up in massive drifts, covering the frozen waters. Then no one would venture onto the snow and risk plunging through hidden ice to certain death.

Even when at its best, like today, the plateau offered hints of its darker side: the stunted trees, bent into grotesque shapes by howling winter winds that came shrieking through the wide valley; the wide cracks in the sun-baked surface crust, fragile and crumbling, areas that grazing animals sensed were best to avoid. The plateau was always ready to lure the unwary away from solid ground towards sudden danger.

Gilbert Noury and his twin, Eddie, knew the plateau as well as most, but even they were constantly alert there, because the plateau was ever-changing, its shifting waters creating new hazards and traps.

Gilbert had elected to return to the plateau with two of the Brandenburgers, leaving his younger-by-ten-minutes brother, Eddie, at the wood yard.

The three men were looking for possible landing sites for the returning Junkers Ju-52. But after a couple of hours, the two Germans seemed finally to have come to the conclusion that Victor Forêt's boast that he had chosen the best place was correct.

The ground on which they stood was one of the flattest parts of the entire plateau. Just as importantly, it was relatively free of water, was solid underfoot and had no hidden pools lurking in crucial parts of what was to become a temporary landing strip.

The two Brandenburgers had spoken mainly to each other, and in German. They had said little to Gilbert unless they had a question for him, and then they spoke in French.

They had listened carefully to his answers, but offered no further conversation.

Gilbert watched them walk the proposed landing strip twice in each direction, looking for any hidden rocks or ruts that might damage the aircraft's undercarriage. They took their time, eyes peeled, knowing that anything missed could mean disaster for the aircraft and its crew.

Then they walked the strip again, this time looking for signs of hidden pools or sink holes. There were a few, but on the edges, far enough from the centre to make landing relatively straightforward for a skilled pilot. And Ju-52 pilots were all extremely experienced in operating in hostile conditions.

After the second close inspection, Gilbert decided to ask the two Germans their names. The soldier who seemed to be in charge smiled for the first time. "We're the Brothers Grimm," he said, laughing.

"Who?" Gilbert said, his face blank.

"You must have heard of us," the soldier continued, still grinning. "We tell fairy stories. I'm Jacob, and my brother there is Wilhelm."

Gilbert turned to the second German. "He's … he's joking isn't he? Pulling my leg?"

The second soldier was stony-faced. "No, he's always deadly serious."

"And we're here to do serious work, so we'd best get on with it," the first soldier said, his smile vanishing. He looked at the grass strip. "The Ju-52 needs about two hundred metres for landing and take-off, so this is good. And there's enough room for the plane to turn into the wind." He turned back towards the narrow road that ran between the tiny villages of Espezel and Bélesta. The lorry was parked there, a hundred metres or so from where they stood. "That's my only concern. We're just a little too visible to anyone who might be passing."

"You don't have to worry about that," Gilbert told him. "The road is almost never used at night; it's hardly used during the day."

The German nodded, apparently convinced. "And you have the landing torches prepared?"

"Exactly as you ordered. They just need putting into place and lighting. But we'll do that when..."

He stopped and all three men looked at the road again.

A blue, open-backed van, belching smoke from its exhaust, was moving quickly towards them from the direction of Bélesta.

"Hardly used, eh?" the soldier said, his eyes fixed on the van.

The vehicle appeared to be passing by without stopping, but just as it reached the lorry, the driver jammed on the brakes and the van bumped to a skidding standstill on the grass at the edge of the road.

The two soldiers exchanged a look and waited. The driver's door opened and the sound of creaking hinges drifted across the plateau.

A man stepped out and stared in their direction. He waved, and they heard him shout. "Eddie, is that you?"

"Shit!" Gilbert breathed. "It's my cousin."

"Get rid of him," the German in charge hissed.

But it was too late. The man was already walking towards them, limping as he strode across the grass. "Or is that Gilbert?" he yelled. "You two should wear signs to give us a chance."

"I'll have to talk to him," Gilbert said quietly to the soldiers.

"I said get rid of him!"

"I can't just tell him to clear off. Look, he's harmless. Thinks he's a bit of a big shot, likes to brag, but it's all talk. He's no trouble, really." He waved at the approaching man. "It's me, Alain: Gilbert. And what's wrong, why are you limping?"

The young man waited to speak until he reached the other three, extending his hand to his cousin. "Gilbert, how are you? What the hell are you doing out here?"

"I'm just…" Gilbert glanced at the two wary Germans and decided that the safest option was to change the subject. "Why the limp, Alain? What happened to your leg?"

The newcomer spat on the ground. "It was that bastard, Victor Forêt."

The two soldier's eyes met again briefly, but they remained silent as the newcomer continued.

"I had an argument with him in the bar. He grabbed

me when I wasn't ready for him. Pushed me, and I tripped; fell onto one of those tables on the terrace. It's just a bruise, that's all. I wasn't ready for him."

Gilbert smiled, trying to keep the conversation away from the men he was with. "And what did you fight over?"

"It didn't get as far as a fight, lucky for him. Just because he got his nose broken playing rugby years ago he thinks he's a tough guy."

"Whereas you really are a tough guy, eh, Alain?" Gilbert said with a laugh that was a bit too forced. "And, anyway, Victor always knows best about rugby."

The newcomer was smaller and slighter than the twins, but had the same dark, curly hair and square jaw. "We didn't argue about rugby," he said, scowling.

"What, then?"

"Victor was going on about how grateful we ought to be to the Germans for getting us out of the war. I told him if that's how he feels, then he's nothing more than a filthy collaborator. That's when it turned nasty."

Gilbert froze. He had no idea of his cousin's sympathies regarding the war; they'd never discussed it.

Gilbert was standing next to the German in charge, but the other soldier, moving like a shadow, had slipped behind Alain. His hand went slowly behind his back as he reached for the pistol tucked into his belt under his jacket. He stared calmly at his colleague, waiting for a signal to take action.

Completely unaware, Alain continued. "But forget about

Victor," he said to his cousin. "You didn't say what you're doing here, Gilbert. And you didn't introduce me to your friends."

"No," Gilbert said, "no, I didn't." He glanced nervously at the man at his side. "This is, er…"

"Pierre," the German said in French as he offered his hand to Alain. "And that's my friend Marcel."

Alain shook hands with the first German and then turned to the second, whose hand was already extended. He smiled and nodded as they shook.

"Judging from your accent you're not from around these parts," Alain said to the man who had introduced himself as Pierre.

"No, we're from over to the west, the other side of Toulouse."

Alain nodded, but didn't look convinced. "So what are you doing up here on the plateau?"

The cover story was prepared. "We've been thinking of bringing some cattle here. Your cousin was kind enough to show us around."

Alain laughed. "Gilbert knows nothing about cattle. If it's grazing land you want you should have come to me. I was born over in Espezel, I know everyone up here. Speak to old Jacques Moutillon, he'll tell you all about grazing rights. I'm on my way there now; I can take you to see him if you want."

"Thanks, but no. We've seen enough, and it's not what we're looking for."

Alain still looked as though he didn't quite believe what he was hearing. "I don't know why you asked Gilbert. All the twins know about is cutting down trees and selling off the wood."

"Yeah, and I'd best get back to the yard," Gilbert said quickly. "I've left Eddie on his own, and you know what he's like – he'd rather sit around all day than do any work."

"I'll come with you," Alain said. "I was going over to the house, to fetch ... to sort a few things, but it can wait. It's been ages since you, me and Eddie had a few beers and a good laugh."

The soldier behind Alain moved his hand towards the back of his jacket again, and this time Gilbert saw the move. Instantly he realized that his cousin was in mortal danger. "No, not today, Alain," he said hurriedly. "We have to get some work done. Maybe sometime next week, eh?"

"Oh, come on, a couple of beers won't hurt you."

"No!" Gilbert spat out the word too loudly and forcefully. "Not today. We don't have time. I'm sorry, Alain."

Alain's face darkened, his eyes narrowing and becoming hostile. "Suit yourself."

Gilbert was desperate to lighten the tense atmosphere. "Next week, eh?" he said brightly.

His cousin hesitated, looking from one stranger to another. He shrugged his shoulders. "Maybe," he said sulkily.

"No, definitely," Gilbert told him. He turned towards the road, took his cousin's arm and pushed him ahead so that he was leading the way back towards the parked vehicles. "You're right; it's been too long. We'll get the beers in and make a night of it, eh?"

The Germans followed. After a few paces, the soldier in charge gave a slight, almost imperceptible shake of his head to his colleague, who nodded and released the hold on the pistol in his belt.

SIX

Hauptmann Kurt Lau was a conscientious officer committed to doing his duty. He was as fiercely loyal to his men as they were to him. They made a formidable team, which was one of the reasons why they had been kept together during an uncertain period for the Brandenburgers.

The entire regiment had moved to northern France the previous year, anticipating a major role in the invasion of Britain. But Operation Sea Lion had been suddenly postponed in September and many said that now it would never happen.

Other units of the regiment had moved on to major conflicts in Yugoslavia and Greece, but Kurt Lau and his team had been detailed a series of small hit and run operations. They were all important, but this one was something special; Lau had been told just enough to be certain of that.

His orders were clear. If the first objective of capturing the target and taking him back to northern France proved impossible, there was only one alternative – the target had to be eliminated. The knowledge he held was judged to be so important that it could not be allowed to pass into enemy hands.

Lau and the soldier driving the stolen Citroën police car were on their way back to the wood yard. The recce had gone smoothly; the house could be approached front and back. They would snatch the target early the following morning, return to the yard, radio headquarters, and as long as weather conditions stayed fair, be picked up by the Ju-52 that same night. It was a simple plan, but Lau was taking nothing for granted. Experience had taught him otherwise.

They were on the long road that snaked up through the forest of Bélesta. The climb was swift and steep, and with each twisting turn they glimpsed sudden falls and deep gorges on either side.

"Good countryside, eh, Erich?" Lau said to the driver. "Reminds me a little of the Black Forest." He laughed. "But not so nice, eh? Not like home."

Lau would never usually address one of his team by his first name, even when they were out of earshot of other serving soldiers. But Erich Steidle was the exception. In his late thirties, Steidle was a good ten years older than Lau. Both men came from the city of Freiburg, in the south-west of Germany, close to the border with France. But while Lau's career before the war had been as a professor of languages at the city's ancient university, Steidle had laboured in the vineyards of both Germany and France, where he had learned his French.

Coincidence had brought the two together in the Brandenburgers, but since then, Steidle, hard and as tough as teak, had taken the younger man under his wing. He was devoted to the officer and protective in an almost fatherly way.

"I'll be glad to get back to the north, sir," Steidle said, manoeuvring the Citroën around another sharp bend. "It's strange here – no sign of the war and no sign of the enemy. At least in the north we know that almost everyone is our enemy."

Lau smiled. "Yes, it is strange here: France, but not France. But the Vichy government likes to think it's in charge of things in the south and we must allow them that." He glanced out at the huge trees. "One day this war will be over, Erich."

"Could be a long time, though, sir."

Steidle turned the vehicle onto the mud track and they bumped past the stacks of piled logs and the house and the chained, barking dog, and drove into the yard.

The lorry had already returned from the plateau and was parked close to the barn. At the sound of the approaching car, another of Lau's men emerged from the house, followed by one of the twins. The twin hung back, but the soldier was waiting by the vehicle as Lau opened the door and stepped out.

Lau frowned. The dog's ferocious barking sounded even louder than it had the previous night.

"Everything go OK on the plateau?" Lau asked the waiting soldier.

"A slight problem, sir."

"Go on."

"Nothing wrong with the landing strip; it's good, just as Monsieur Beergut told us. We double checked everything."

"But?"

"A man turned up." He gestured with his head towards the twin standing by the house. "A cousin of theirs. He was curious, had plenty to say, a bit full of himself. I used the cover story, but I'm not sure he was fooled."

"Will he come here?"

The soldier shook his head. "The twin told him they were busy for the next few days."

Lau stared towards the forest, thinking over what he had heard.

"And there's one more thing, sir," the soldier continued. "The man had been fighting."

"Why does that concern us?"

"He'd been fighting with our friend, Monsieur Beergut. At his bar in Lavelanet. Sounds as though he can't keep his mouth shut, even when he's not drinking his own beer."

The dog was still barking as the twin approached Lau. "And which one are you?"

"Gilbert, but that doesn't matter."

"Perhaps I'll be able to tell the difference by the time we leave."

"I doubt it," Gilbert shrugged. "One of your men almost shot my cousin this morning. I watched him go for his pistol."

"But he didn't shoot him."

"No, but I knew that one wrong word from my cousin and he'd have been lying dead out there on the plateau. It wasn't necessary, Alain's no trouble, I just had to talk to him."

"Then let's hope you convinced him to stay away for the next couple of days."

"Look, we're helping you," Gilbert said angrily. "We're not your enemies and we're not involved in your war. And you couldn't be doing any of this without us."

Lau's voice softened. "Gilbert, let me assure you that I have no wish to kill anyone." He glanced towards where he knew the dog was tethered. "Anyone, or anything."

SEVEN

The mood around the table was tense, the air heavy with expectation.

Henri had summoned them all, but had refused to say why until everyone was present. Now they were: his wife, Hélène; his daughter, Josette; Didier and Paul.

Hélène, dressed all in black, as she had been since the death of her son the previous year, looked pale and anxious. She had never fully recovered from the blow of losing Venant.

"We're all here, Papa," Josette said, "as you insisted. So why all the hurry?"

"Because Paul is leaving us."

"Yes, he told us that this morning," Josette said impatiently. She flashed a hostile look at Paul. They hadn't spoken since her outburst in Henri's office, and if Paul had been hoping that Josette's temper might have eased since she got home, then he was mistaken. She looked as furious now, sitting at the dining room table, as she had when she had stormed away from her desk earlier in the day.

"But since this morning there have been developments," Henri said. "I've made radio contact with London twice. And the outcome is that they want Paul back there urgently."

"How urgently?" Paul asked before Josette could speak.

"They're not prepared to wait for a second attempt at crossing the mountains. It would take too long, and even after that, you might not get to London for months."

"So what is happening?"

"They're sending an aeroplane for you."

"A plane!"

Henri nodded in response. He looked almost as surprised by his news as everyone else.

"But they can't send a plane from England," Paul said. "It's too far. Where would it land? Where would it refuel?"

"It's not coming from England. A light aircraft is flying from somewhere in the north of Portugal."

"But Portugal is a neutral country," Josette said.

"We have sympathizers there."

"But then what?" Paul asked, hardly believing his ears.

"You'll fly to Portugal, to a landing strip near the coast. A British submarine will be waiting offshore to take you to Britain."

This time no one spoke, but all eyes were on Paul. He looked stunned. "How soon?"

"A few days at most. The submarine is on its way, and the British and their friends in Portugal and Spain are making their plans. We won't be told the operational details."

"Because we don't need to know."

The "need to know" rule was second nature to them all by now.

"Exactly," Henri said. "But, yes, the aircraft will obviously have to stop to refuel on both legs of the journey, probably somewhere near the border between Spain and France. We'll receive further instructions as they come through, but we must be ready to move at a moment's notice."

"And where will I be picked up from?"

Henri shook his head. "For now you know as much as I do."

Didier gave Paul a reassuring smile. "It's what you wanted, Paul. And we'll do what we can to help."

Paul's mind was racing. Only the previous evening his head had been full of dreams of eventually returning to England to join the war effort. It seemed this was to become reality much sooner than he could ever have imagined.

He was sitting next to Hélène, where he always sat when they were eating. He knew it was the chair her son had used, but Hélène had seemed to take comfort from Paul's presence at her side.

She reached across and put one hand on his on the tabletop. "It sounds dangerous," she said to Henri.

"Yes, but Paul is accustomed to danger now."

"And it is his choice to go," Josette said, not looking at

Paul. "But why, Papa, why is there this urgency to get him back to Britain?"

Henri considered for a moment. "Paul told me something when we spoke this morning, something about his father that the British are very anxious to know. Something that could help the whole war effort."

Josette looked briefly at Paul and then back at her father. "Then why can't you just radio them the information?"

"Far too risky. Messages are intercepted and decoded. Paul must pass on what he knows in person."

Josette turned to Paul. "Another secret? Something else you decided not to let us in on until now?"

"It isn't like that," Paul said quickly. "I only realized it myself this morning when I was talking to your father. Something my father had told me."

"Oh, how convenient. So what is this great secret?"

"No!" Henri said, before Paul could reply. "Don't say any more."

"But he's told you, Papa," Josette snapped.

Henri shook his head. "No, Josette. All Paul has told me is that he thinks he knows the *whereabouts* of vital information his father had. And that's all I've passed on to London. I don't know what that information is and neither does Paul. He knows where the information is hidden, and *that* is what he must tell the British. In person."

Suddenly Josette didn't care about being angry any more. All that mattered was that Paul was going to leave very soon. And she didn't want it to happen.

"But what about everyone at the factory?" she said to Henri as panic tightened her chest. "What will we tell them?"

"We use Paul's cover story; the one he's had all along. We say he decided after all that he doesn't want to make a career in the textile industry and has returned to his family north of Lyon."

"And Gra-mere?" Josette was searching desperately for reasons to delay Paul's imminent departure. "He can't just disappear without saying goodbye to her."

Henri thought for a moment. "Yes, you should see my mother, Paul; she's become very fond of you, as we all have. She'll know to say nothing about this to anyone, so visit her tomorrow and say your farewells."

"I will," Paul said.

"But…"

Everyone turned to look at Josette, but she could think of nothing else to say. She shook her head and stared down at the table.

Henri sighed. "It's incredible. In a matter of days they'll swoop in, pick you up and you'll be gone. And then who knows when we'll see you again."

Hélène seemed to be on the verge of tears. She squeezed Paul's hand, got up and left the room.

"They've given the operation a codename for radio contact," Henri said as the door closed. "You should know it,

57

Didier, in case you have to take over."

"Why would I need to take over?"

Henri shrugged. "Just in case – the codename is *Eagle*."

EIGHT

The warm spring day had turned into another chilly night, but sitting in the darkness beneath the vine-covered pergola on the back of the house, Josette was oblivious to the cold.

There was enough starlight to make out most of the walled garden: the trees and shrubs, the bulbs poking through the grass, the old iron gate at the far end that was always closed but never locked.

It was all so familiar; Josette had spent the entire seventeen years of her life living in that house. And the town of Lavelanet. It suddenly seemed a small world now that Paul would be flying away, probably forever.

The house was quiet. Josette knew her parents had gone to bed, but had no idea where Paul was. She got up from the painted metal chair, wandered aimlessly over the paving slabs of the terrace and walked further into the garden.

Soft footsteps sounded behind her and she turned to see Paul approaching. He was carrying one of her warm jackets. Josette smiled. There was no anger now, or panic, just an overwhelming feeling of deep sadness.

"I saw you out here; thought you must be cold," Paul said, handing over the jacket.

"A bit, I suppose," Josette answered, putting on the jacket and fastening the buttons. She hesitated before speaking again. "Paul, who do you think killed Gaston Rouzard?"

Paul gave a short laugh. "That's the last thing I thought you'd ask me now."

Josette smiled. "You thought I'd start complaining again about you leaving us. But I won't, not any more. And I'm sorry for getting so angry; I think I understand why you want to go now."

"I want to go but… I don't want to leave you. Any of you. It's just that…"

"I know. I'll miss you, Paul."

"And I'll miss you. Maybe one day…"

"Don't say it," Josette interrupted. "Let's wait and see."

They walked slowly back to the pergola and sat on the garden chairs.

"You didn't answer my question," Josette said.

"About Gaston? I don't know. I've thought about it often, but I've never really come up with an answer."

"Try again."

"But why?"

"Because when you've gone, I want us – Papa and Didier and me – to do more for the Resistance. Try to recruit again, become more organized. We've got lazy, even Papa. It's because we think there's nothing we can do. But we can. We must."

Paul considered his words before replying. "It won't be easy, Josette. There hasn't been much enthusiasm for the Resistance up until now."

"Then we have to change things. We have to be ready for the Germans when they come, and they *will* come, Paul."

"Maybe. But the trouble is…" He stopped, not wanting to spark another argument.

"What?"

"Nothing."

"Come on, what were you going to say?"

"You won't like it."

"Well, now that you're leaving, it doesn't really matter, does it? Please, tell me."

Josette shivered and pulled up the collar of her jacket against the cold as Paul leaned closer. "I was going to say that the trouble is, from what I've seen, there are too many people in this part of France who haven't decided whose side they're on."

Paul was expecting a familiar explosion of outrage from Josette. It didn't come.

"I know," she said softly. "They sit on the fence, waiting to see which way the war goes before making up their mind. They're not thinking about what's right, just about what's right for them. It makes me ashamed, Paul."

"Maybe we shouldn't be too hard on them," Paul said,

surprised at Josette's unusually subdued response. "Maybe it's always been like this when one country invades another. Some people just want an easy life, no trouble. And not everyone wants to be a hero of the Resistance."

Josette's fiery temper returned in an instant. "Well, I do! And I will be! And I'll start by tracking down our enemies here. And that includes whoever killed Gaston Rouzard, and denied me the pleasure!"

"That's more like the Josette Mazet I know," Paul said, smiling. "But it won't be easy: we don't have much to go on."

"But we do. We know Gaston and Yvette Bigou were working with the Andorrans who killed Jean-Pierre and almost killed us."

Paul nodded. "And we know they were doing it for money, not just because they wanted to destroy our Resistance group. And we know someone silenced Yvette because we'd discovered her involvement."

"Exactly," Josette said, warming to the detective work. "But it wasn't Gaston, because he was drunk in Chalabre that night. He didn't get back to Lavelanet until the following morning, the day he was shot. Which means that someone else killed Yvette and then killed Gaston. But why?"

"Because he was part of the operation, too, and was afraid that Gaston would give him away."

"Or her," Josette said pointedly. "But the point is, we're

not just searching for a traitor, we're after a murderer, a cold-blooded killer." She thought for a moment, then peered through the gloom at Paul. "Or at least, I am."

They fell silent. Their feelings for each other had grown stronger in the months since Paul's arrival but neither had ever quite managed to put those feelings into words. One kiss was as far as their romance had gone, and that had been way back when Paul was about to leave for the first time. Since then, the kiss had never been mentioned and never been repeated. While in every other way they were strong and courageous, when it came to each other their courage seemed to desert them both.

The night had darkened, clouds moving across the sky to block the starlight. Paul edged closer, making sure Josette could see his face as he spoke. "When I've gone, you will be careful, won't you?"

Josette answered in little more than a whisper. "I'll be careful. But I will get him. Or her." She stood up. "Let's go in. I have a feeling tomorrow will be a busy day for us both."

They went to the back door and as Paul started to open it, Josette stopped him. He turned to look at her and she kissed him lightly on the lips.

"Come back one day, Paul," she said, then pulled open the door and went quickly inside.

NINE

Day Three

Someone was knocking on the front door. Hammering, pounding, constant and heavy. A voice was shouting: "Open up! Open up!"

For a few confused seconds, Paul thought he was dreaming, but then realized what was happening. They'd come for him. At the very last moment, just as he was about to escape to freedom, he was going to be arrested and taken in.

It was too cruel: heartbreaking. In those agonizing seconds, he saw himself being dragged off and spirited away to Belgium or northern France to be interrogated, before suffering the same fate as his parents. But as his thoughts cleared, he swore to himself that he wouldn't be taken without a fight. He leapt from his bed, dragged on his clothes and yanked open the bedroom door.

The pounding on the front door grew even louder as Paul came face to face with a grim-faced Henri and a terrified-looking Hélène as they emerged from their bedroom. Then Josette came out of her room.

"What's happening?" Josette said, her eyes wide but

defiant. "Who is it, what do we do?"

"It must be the police," Paul answered. "They've come for me. I'll try to make a run for it out the back way."

"No, Paul," Henri said, "they'll be armed and they'll have put someone at the back too."

"Should we open the shutters, see how many there are?"

As always, the shutters on the house had been closed the previous night. Paul himself had locked the one on the back door before going up to bed. Closed shutters meant security, and no one outside seeing into the house. But it also meant that no one on the inside could see exactly who was hammering at the door. Or how many of them were out there.

"We'll open the door and bluff it out," Henri said. "There's no other choice. Paul has papers; we'll have to hope they pass as genuine."

Paul's forged identity card and work and travel permits had always been accepted, but they had never been scrutinized too closely.

"Let me go down," Paul said. "It's me they've come for."

"It's my house," Henri said firmly. "I shall open the door."

Followed by Paul, Henri went to the staircase and then looked back at Hélène and Josette. "Stay here."

At the bottom of the stairs, the pounding and shouting sounded louder still. But the noise stopped completely as Henri pulled back the sturdy bolts at the top and bottom of the door. He glanced briefly at Paul, smiled reassuringly, then turned the large black key that had remained in the lock overnight, just as it always did.

The mechanism of the ancient lock clunked loudly, breaking the sudden silence. Henri pushed down the door handle and slowly pulled open the heavy door.

And then he stared. So did Paul.

Staring back at them were two men. One was tall and slim and looked to be in his mid-thirties. He had a shock of wild black hair, his thin face was drawn and haggard and his eyes were dark with worry. He wore a loose-fitting, crumpled old suit with a white shirt that was open at the neck.

The other man was in his late sixties. His face was flushed and what hair remained was grey and sparse. Dressed in baggy fawn-coloured trousers and a rough working shirt and jacket, he looked as though he might have come from the fields.

Neither man seemed remotely like a gendarme or a soldier. And both men looked scared.

For a few seconds, all four stood bewildered in the early morning light, just staring.

Then the younger newcomer spoke. "It's my wife – they've taken my wife!"

Henri hesitated, his brow creased. "Your wife? Who's taken your wife? And who are you? Why have you come here?"

"That was my idea, Monsieur Mazet," the older man said. "We didn't know where else to go."

"You know me?" Henri said.

The man lowered his voice. "I know of you. We're from Bélesta, and … well, I've … I've heard things, over the past year. People talk. Say things. You know."

"No, I don't know. And I don't know what you're talking about."

"About … about a Resistance group. Here in Lavelanet. Your name was mentioned."

Henri said nothing, fearing that he might be being drawn into a trap.

"There's no one in Bélesta we could go to," the man continued. "So we came here." He pointed back to the road. "In my old car."

Henri remained silent, forcing the man to go on. "I have a relative who works in your factory."

"Who?" Paul asked, impatient to know exactly what the men were expecting. "What's his name?"

"It's Joseph Argoud," the man answered, still looking at Henri. "He's been with you for years. My wife's younger brother."

Henri nodded, but said nothing.

"My name is Antoine Granel. You can ask Joseph about me, or anyone in Bélesta, they'll vouch for me. But my young friend here needs your help."

Again, Henri waited, giving himself time to think before replying. "If he needs help, then he must go to the police," he said at last.

"But I can't go to the police," the younger man said

loudly, his face desperate with worry. "It was the police who took my wife away."

Paul and Henri exchanged a look.

"Why? Why did they do that?" Henri asked.

"They were looking for me," the man said. "But I wasn't there, so they took my wife, and I've no idea where they've taken her."

"Please?" Antoine Granel said to Henri. "Will you at least give us a chance to explain?"

Again, Henri hesitated. Then he and Paul turned as they heard a creak on the staircase. Hélène and Josette had made their way down the stairs.

"Ask our visitors to come in, Henri," Hélène said. "You can't leave them standing on the doorstep like that."

"But, Hélène," Henri replied, "we know nothing about—"

"Ask them in, Henri," Hélène said, more assertively this time. "I'll make coffee while you go and dress. If you stay there, the whole neighbourhood will hear your conversation."

TEN

"I don't sleep well, I've always had trouble sleeping."
The younger of the two men had finally introduced
himself as Max Bernard. He put down his coffee cup and
tapped his head with one finger. "Too much going on up
here all the time, thinking about my work."

They were gathered in the sitting room. The shutters
were open now, and the morning light was warming the
room. Henri had dressed in his usual workday suit, Josette
had flung on whatever had come to hand and Paul was still
in the clothes he had dragged on as he heard the thunderous
knocking on the front door.

Hélène made coffee and then left them to it, knowing that
she would learn the details of their conversation soon
enough.

"Please go on, Monsieur Bernard," Henri said, satisfied
that the visitors posed no threat.

"Max: call me Max."

Henri nodded. "Please go on, Max."

"My wife needs her sleep; when I'm restless I disturb

her. Often I get up in the early hours and walk, usually by the river. It's quiet; I can think. When I return, if it's still dark, I'm sometimes tired enough to sleep for an hour or two before breakfast. That's how it was this morning, but just as I went to turn the corner to our street I saw them. Well, I heard them first."

"Heard who?"

"The gendarmes. Something made me stop; I was hidden from their sight by the wall of a house. I peered around the corner. It was still dark, but I could see enough. Two of them, and my wife. And she was..." Tears welled in the corners of his eyes. "She was crying; saying I was away and wouldn't be back for days. I should have gone to help, but I didn't. I hid behind the wall and stayed there until I heard their car drive away."

"You couldn't have done anything, Max," Antoine Granel told him. "Better to come to me so that we could both try to get help."

"But your wife needed help then," Josette said, her face angry. "I wouldn't have—"

"Josette, please!" Henri said. "Listen to what Monsieur Berna— to what Max has to say before you go jumping to conclusions."

"No, your daughter's right," Max said. "Julia did need my help. But you see, we knew this might happen one day; that they would come for me. But Julia always said that it was most important that I stay free, even if she was taken."

"Well, that's ridicu—!" Josette fell silent as she saw her father glaring at her. She looked over at Paul, who also gave her a warning look.

"Perhaps you can explain what you mean by that, Max?" Henri asked gently.

"Yes. Yes, of course. I'm a scientist, a physicist. Before the war I was working in Germany; research, with some of the very best they had. I was considered one of the best. But after Hitler came to power, we decided we should leave while we could. I'm Jewish, you see. We came home to France. Paris first, and then when Paris became unsafe last year, we travelled here, helped by friends along the way."

He paused for a moment and took a drink of coffee, lifting the cup in both hands. They were shaking.

Paul took the opportunity to look at Josette. She was staring back at him. They realized that Max and Julia Bernard might very well have had a similar journey through France as Paul's, probably with similarly heart-stopping moments.

"We managed to get false papers," Max continued, "and we have a little money. We hoped we might hide away quietly until the war is over."

"So the police came for you this morning because you're Jewish?" Paul asked.

"No, I don't believe it was that."

"What, then?"

"They want me for what I know. For my knowledge. It appears that the Nazis are not as concerned about a person's race or ethnic background if they can be of particular use to them. And I can."

"In what way?" Henri asked. "If you don't mind telling us."

Max finished his coffee. His hands were still trembling. "They know I can help them build a nuclear weapon."

"A what?" Josette said. "What is that?"

"A bomb."

"But they have bombs. Hundreds of bombs. Thousands."

The scientist shook his head. "Not like this. At the moment no such weapon exists. But it will, and before too long. The Americans, the British, the Germans, probably the Russians, too, they're all racing to build it, and one day someone will succeed. And when they do…" His voice trailed away.

"But this bomb?" Paul asked. "What sort of weapon will it be?"

Max sighed heavily. "Like nothing you have ever imagined. A bomb that will not just destroy a building, but whole towns, entire cities. A single bomb capable of killing hundreds of thousands, perhaps millions."

"But … but that's impossible," Josette breathed. "It can't be."

"It will happen," Max said, "I promise you. But I won't be part of it – for anyone, the Germans, the Americans, anyone. When I left Germany I swore I would never again help develop such a monstrous weapon. But that means nothing to the Germans. That's why they've come for me."

"Germans?" Paul said. "But you said it was the police. Two gendarmes in a police car."

"Perhaps," Max said. "But I was very close, and voices travel in the morning air, even softly spoken voices. I'm certain I heard one of them speaking German as they bundled my wife into the car."

Paul felt his heart thudding in his chest as Antoine Granel leaned across to his friend. "And tell them about the car; where it went."

"Oh, yes, the car. When they drove away, the car didn't head towards Lavelanet, as you would expect, or even in the opposite direction towards Puivert. They crossed the river and headed up towards the forest of Bélesta and the Plateau de Sault."

"Now why would gendarmes go that way?" Antoine said to Henri. "There's nothing up there but trees and cows. Will you help, monsieur? Will you and your Resistance group find Julia and help us get her back?"

"Well…" Henri said slowly. "We're not really…"

"Of course we'll help," Paul said quickly. "That's what we're here for, to fight the enemies of France."

The elderly man smiled at Paul. "Excuse me for saying this, monsieur, but you look very … very young for … this sort of work."

"Everyone…" Paul glanced briefly at Henri. "*Almost* everyone in our group is very young. But we're all experienced, we've all seen action and we're all prepared for further action." He turned back to Henri. "Isn't that right, Henri?"

"Well…"

"And how many are you?" the elderly man asked before Henri could reply.

"We prefer to keep that information to ourselves," Paul told him. "It's safest that you don't know. What you don't know, you can't tell anyone else."

Antoine nodded and shrugged his shoulders, appearing to be impressed.

Paul turned to Max. "Did you go back into your house?"

"No, I went straight to Antoine's. He said we should come here and not go into the house in case the gendarmes returned."

"Or in case they're still there," Paul said.

"But I saw them leave, with my wife."

"You saw two of them leave; you don't know how many arrived."

This time even Henri looked impressed. "He's right. They could still be there, waiting for you to walk into a trap."

Paul was thinking quickly as he got to his feet. "Henri, if Monsieur Granel has heard rumours about you and the Resistance, then others must have heard them too. We need to get Max somewhere safe before we have a visit from the gendarmes, or from anyone else. If you organize that, I'll go and speak to Didier."

"And I'll go with him," Josette said, getting up from her chair.

"But…"

"There's no time to lose, Henri," Paul said, walking to the door, with Josette following. "We must act now."

"But—"

They were out of the room before Henri had the chance to stop them. Grabbing their coats, they left the house to walk to the factory, where they knew Didier would soon be arriving for work.

They strode quickly and in silence, side-by-side, each assessing what they'd heard and thrilled at the thought that they were at last taking some positive action, although right then, neither had the remotest idea what that action would be.

"Do you believe what he said?" Josette asked eventually.

"About what?"

"That bomb? That terrible nuclear thing?"

"Of course I believe him. I remember my father talking about the possibility of something like it."

They were nearing the factory when Josette spoke again. "You didn't give Papa a chance to say no to Max back there."

"We couldn't say no. This is our chance to do something

important, Josette. It's exactly what we've been waiting for."

"Yes, but aren't you forgetting something?"

"Forgetting what?"

"There's a plane coming to pick you up and a submarine waiting off the coast of Portugal. You'll be gone from here in a few days."

ELEVEN

Julia Bernard was not a woman who was easily frightened, but she was terrified now. It had all happened so quickly. One moment she'd been sleeping peacefully, and the next, two of them were in the house – in the bedroom – ordering her to get dressed and demanding to know Max's whereabouts.

Even then Julia thought fast. They had allowed her a little privacy as she pulled on her clothes, so by the time she faced them again she was ready with a story. It was thin, but it was all she could think of. Max was away for a few days, visiting a friend in Perpignan. She didn't know why she said Perpignan; it could have been anywhere. They didn't believe her, she knew that, but at least the man in charge had not yelled and threatened like the others. And at least Max had not arrived back to be captured.

But when Julia was bundled into the car and driven away, one of the men had remained at the house. All Julia could do now was pray that a neighbour had seen or heard something and would warn her husband before he walked into a trap.

She was in a locked room in a house somewhere deep in the forest of Bélesta. It was gloomy, dusty and dark. The shutters were closed and Julia had been ordered not to touch them. Outside a dog was barking; it had been barking ever since they'd arrived. But how long ago was that? Julia didn't know. An hour? Two hours? More? She didn't know. Every second seemed like an eternity.

The door creaked open and a man stood in the doorway, silhouetted by the light from the room beyond. He'd been at the house; he was in charge.

"Will you come in here, please?" he asked quietly, in French.

Julia got to her feet, her heart thudding. There was no point in disobeying his request. She would do as they asked, but she was determined to tell them nothing.

The man stood aside as she stepped past him into the other room. It was much bigger: a sprawling, heavily beamed room with sagging armchairs and a dark oak dresser that covered most of one wall. The shutters were open and Julia could just see through the grease-smeared windows that outside the sun was shining.

There was an upright chair in the centre of the room. An older man stood behind it. He'd been at the house too.

"Sit here, please," he said. He too spoke quietly, but there was no mistaking the menace in his voice.

It chilled Julia; again she did as she was instructed. She could sense the man behind her, not moving. She could feel his eyes boring into the back of her head. She forced herself to focus on the man in front of her. He was watching too, but his eyes were softer, kinder perhaps. But Julia told herself not to be fooled.

He touched the lapel of the military jacket he wore. "By now you will have realized, Madame Bernard, that we are not, as we appear, French gendarme officers."

"You're Germans," Julia answered, her voice wavering slightly. "I heard you speak when your friend pushed me into the car."

"I'm sorry if you were hurt," the German said, his eyes flicking for a moment to the man behind Julia. "I have no wish to hurt a woman; I have no particular wish to hurt anyone."

Outside, the dog continued to bark.

"My name is Lau, Hauptmann Kurt Lau," the officer said, frowning and glancing towards the window. "I'm here to escort you and your husband back to Germany as quickly as possible. Where is he, Madame Bernard?"

Julia swallowed. "I told you before, he's in Perpignan, visiting an old friend."

"And the name of this friend?"

"I don't know."

Lau raised his eyebrows. "An old friend, but you don't know his name?"

"He's my husband's friend, not mine. They were at university together, I think."

"Ah, you think."

79

Julia said nothing.

"And when will your husband return, Madame Bernard?"

"I don't know. Three days; four, perhaps. He didn't say for certain."

Lau continued to stare at Julia, his eyes unblinking. "Madame Bernard, I said I have no wish to hurt you, and that's perfectly true. None of my men would choose to harm you, either." He looked briefly at Erich Steidle, who stood like a statue behind Julia. "But my colleague is skilled in interrogation techniques, some of them not very pleasant. I suggest that for your own good you stop lying now and tell me exactly where your husband is."

Julia's blood froze. For a moment she was ready to burst into tears and beg the German not to hurt her. But she sucked in a halting breath and spoke bravely. "As I said before, I don't know exactly where my husband is."

The radio operator had sent a simple message to base. There was an unexpected slight delay in the mission. The pick-up for the return flight could not go ahead tonight.

Lau was irritated but calm; he wouldn't allow himself to become angry. Anger was not good or useful in a soldier. It affected clear thinking and decision-making, and Lau needed to think clearly and make firm decisions.

Once the radio transmitter was shut down, Lau sent the operator outside to join two more of his men who were keeping watch for unexpected visitors. The sixth member of the team was back at the Bernards' house in Bélesta, waiting.

Lau and Steidle were in the kitchen smoking strong cigarettes.

The officer took a long drag on his cigarette and frowned. The barking dog was only increasing his irritation. "Where are the twins?" he asked gruffly.

"Cutting down trees," Steidle told him with a shrug of his shoulders. "Or chopping logs, or whatever it is they do."

"Why don't they take that animal with them?"

"They say it's meant to warn them if strangers turn up when they're away from the yard. The sound of barking travels for miles."

Lau sighed. "I've noticed."

"Do you believe the woman, sir?"

Lau had given Julia time to think but warned her that she didn't have long.

"Of course not. Do you?"

Steidle shook his head. "Shall I question her?"

"Not yet. If she's harmed, her husband is far less likely to cooperate when we do track him down."

"Where do you think he is, sir?"

"Not in Perpignan, for sure. He's close. Maybe he did go visiting, but only overnight. He'll be back."

"Should I put another man in the house?"

Lau nodded. "When we relieve Werner. He can cope if Bernard returns before then."

"They won't be in gendarme uniforms, sir. Unless we give them ours."

"No, the uniforms will become a liability if we're seen in them too often. The locals will start asking questions. Once more and then we'll switch to civilian clothes over our own uniforms."

"And the police vehicle?"

"We'll use it once more, that's all."

"But we don't have another car, sir."

"Then we'll get one if it becomes necessary!" Lau snapped. He sighed and looked at Steidle. "I'm sorry, Erich. It's that bloody dog; the howling is beginning to drive me crazy."

"It's all right, sir," Steidle said. "I understand."

The officer stubbed out his cigarette in the tin lid that served as an ashtray and glanced around the room. It was grubby, untidy, and even more dilapidated in daylight than beneath the dull lamps of night.

The isolated position meant there was no electricity and no telephone. Apart from radio contact with headquarters, Lau and his team were cut off from the outside world. The operation was not proving as simple as he had anticipated.

"I still believe we'll take Bernard today," he said. "Then we can call in the plane and be away from here tomorrow night." He checked his watch. "And if Bernard is coming home today he'll be back by midday. Frenchmen never miss their lunch."

TWELVE

Rudi Werner was bored. Sitting straight-backed in an upright chair, he had read the spine of every book on the sagging shelves in the sitting room at the back of Max and Julia Bernard's house. First he read them all silently and then he read them aloud, practising his far from perfect French.

He reached the final book on the bottom shelf and, rather than go back to the top shelf and start yet again, he took out his Walther P38 pistol. It was cold in his hand. Cold but comfortable.

Werner liked weapons, particularly small arms: the pistol, the rifle, the submachine-gun. He was good with them all, and even better with the stick grenade. He could throw a stick grenade a very long way.

He examined the pistol. It was new, and he preferred it to his previous pistol, the old Luger P08. The Walther P38 was a little smaller and lighter and, in the right hands, was accurate at up to fifty metres. Werner released the eight-round magazine and checked the weapon for dust. It was immaculate, as always. And ready for action, as was Werner.

He clipped the magazine back into its housing and studied the pistol closely. Perfectly balanced and weighted, it was a precision killing machine. Just like Werner. He glanced at his watch: 11.35. They would come to relieve him soon.

Werner didn't enjoy being in France and he wasn't particularly enjoying this mission; it was too … passive.

Werner wanted to go to England, to be part of the invasion. He was convinced the invasion would still happen, no matter what the doubters said. Werner dreamed of marching triumphantly up Pall Mall among the ranks of proud German soldiers when the ultimate victory was won.

He was daydreaming about this victory march through the streets of London when he heard the key slip into the lock of the front door. Before it had even turned, he had moved noiselessly to the connecting wall between the sitting room and the equally small kitchen and dining area at the front of the house.

He pressed his back against the wall and raised the Walther so that it nestled softly against his chest. Werner smiled. Bernard was back, just as Hauptmann Lau had predicted. He would take him, no trouble. And if Bernard gave him any trouble at all, he would be sorry. Very sorry.

The front door swung open and Werner waited.

Bernard didn't call out. Why would he? He was

expecting his wife to be there as usual.

Werner heard the door close and then footsteps. Bernard was crossing the room. The connecting door between the two rooms was open.

Werner silently moved the pistol away from his chest into a comfortable firing position. His index finger was on the trigger but applying no pressure.

The approaching footsteps stopped.

Werner frowned; perhaps Bernard was suspicious after all. But then the footsteps began again and Werner made ready to terrify the target with a shouted command to halt.

But the word froze on his lips.

It wasn't Bernard. It was a small, plump, elderly woman, wearing a blue and white checked housecoat over a black dress.

She saw Werner, and the pistol aimed at her heart, and her eyes bulged. An ear-piercing scream escaped from her gaping mouth, and before Werner had the chance to order her to stop she had fainted and was lying at his feet.

"Shit!" Werner breathed.

"You'd better come away from the window, Antoine," Paul said as they watched the police car cruise slowly past and come to a standstill outside the Bernard house further down the street.

Four men got out, two of them dressed as gendarmes and two in plain clothes.

"They're not from around here," Antoine Granel said.

"They don't even look French," Didier added.

"They're Germans," Antoine said. "Max was right."

They had travelled quickly to Bélesta, Antoine leading the way in his ancient Renault, with Paul and Didier following on Didier's motorbike. Even at the snail's pace at which Antoine drove, the eight-kilometre journey took just fifteen minutes.

Back in Lavelanet, Paul had come up with the idea of watching the Bernard house, reasoning that if someone was waiting for Max, he would have to be relieved at some point. Even if the house were empty, Julia's abductors would surely return for another attempt to find Max.

And Paul had been proved right. As he watched, the four men took a cursory look up and down the deserted street and then went quickly into the house.

"My Rosalie, my poor Rosalie," Antoine said, turning away from the window. "I should have forbidden her to go over there."

"I don't think that would have stopped her," Paul said. "She was very determined."

"She's always been brave," Antoine continued. "And an actress, such an actress. I'm always telling her she should have been on the stage."

Antoine's wife, Rosalie, had volunteered to go across to the Bernard house to discover if anyone was lying in wait. She kept a spare key for emergencies and said that if necessary she would say she was the cleaner paying her regular weekly visit.

It seemed like a good idea to Paul and Didier at the time, but when Rosalie didn't emerge soon after going into the house, they began to have their doubts. And now the police car had arrived.

"I'm scared," Antoine said. "She's old, you know, older than me. And I'm nearly seventy. I must go over."

"That could make the situation worse," Paul said. "Wait a little longer, please."

"But they might hurt her."

Paul risked a look through the window. "I don't think so; they've got no reason to hurt her. And anyway, from what I saw, I think your wife can look after herself."

THIRTEEN

The twins stood in gloomy silence watching their dog devour scraps of fatty meat and leftovers from their own lunchtime meal. The huge mongrel licked the tin bowl clean and then lapped noisily at the fresh water Eddie had poured into a second tin.

The twins had never bothered giving the animal a name, but that didn't mean they didn't care about it. They did: they liked the dog, but it wasn't a pet. It was a working animal, doing its job, keeping watch.

It was docile when the twins were nearby, but only then. The twins could approach without fear, but no one else. Any unfamiliar sound would provoke deep, ferocious barking, while the merest sight or smell of a stranger would see the animal bare its fangs and prepare to attack.

But with the twins, the dog was different. They didn't offer any affection, but they fed it regularly and made sure its wooden kennel was dry and draught free. And in the depths of winter, when the snow was thick on the ground, the dog was allowed into the house at night, where it slept by the stove before returning to its work place in the morning.

Finishing the water, the animal lifted its head and looked at Eddie, who, without a word, refilled the tin bowl from a can he had carried over from the house. The twins usually said little while they were at work. By the time they left the house they knew exactly what had to be done, so they saved most of their conversation for the evenings.

And besides, they were twins, and like many sets of twins they had an almost telepathic understanding. Both had been thinking a lot that morning, and their thoughts had been along similar lines.

"I didn't like seeing them drag the woman into the house," said Eddie, breaking the silence.

"I know," Gilbert answered. He watched the dog lap up the second bowl of water before continuing. "But they didn't hurt her."

"How do we know that? For certain? We've been working all morning."

"The one who stayed behind, the radio operator, he told me she hasn't been hurt."

"And you believe him?"

Gilbert hesitated before replying. "He said they've given her food. And coffee."

The dog looked from one twin to the other, as though following their conversation. He shook himself, and padded over to Eddie to stand at his side.

"I didn't think about this when Forêt asked us to help," Eddie said.

"Of course you didn't, you just thought about the money. Like I did."

"I don't like this, Gilbert, it doesn't seem right. Forêt said they were coming to pick up a wanted man. That's all. I thought he meant he'd be some sort of criminal. And he didn't say anything about the man's wife."

"Maybe he didn't know."

"And what if they don't find the husband, the one they really want? What will they do with the woman then?"

Gilbert glanced over towards the house. "It's got nothing to do with us, Eddie."

"You think they'll take her back to Germany without the husband?"

"They'll let her go if she's no use to them."

Eddie stared at the ground. "Or kill her and bury her somewhere in the forest."

Gilbert thought back to the previous day on the plateau, when their cousin, Alain, had come perilously close to being shot simply for being in the wrong place at the wrong time. "We won't let them kill her."

"Oh, and how are we supposed to stop them? There are six of them and two of us."

Gilbert turned and stared at the house again. "There's only one of them in there now."

FOURTEEN

The five Germans stood in a ragged semicircle, looking down at Rosalie Granel, who was sprawled on the small sofa in the sitting room, a glass of water in one hand and a sheet of paper, with which she was fanning her face, in the other.

Hauptmann Lau, Steidle, Werner and the two soldiers who had called themselves the Brothers Grimm had combined to lift her fairly gently from the floor, settle her on the chair and fetch her the water.

Now they just stared, limp apologetic smiles on their faces, as they waited for her to speak.

"It was a shock," she gasped eventually, "such a shock. That big man there," she aimed at Werner with the hand holding the glass, "and the gun, pointed at my heart. I was certain he was going to shoot me."

She shivered and rested the sheet of paper over her heart. "I can feel it pounding," she said dramatically, staring at Lau, who was closest. "My heart. Pounding," she repeated for emphasis. "I was certain I was going to have a heart attack." Her voice quivered and she pointed at Werner again. "If he didn't shoot me first. And then, everything went dark and I knew nothing more until you lifted me from the floor."

Lau, who spoke almost perfect French, had indicated to his men that he would do the talking. "We're so sorry, terribly sorry, madame. We had no idea that you would be arriving."

"But I'm always here at this time, every week," Rosalie told him. "To do the cleaning. For Julia."

"Oh, I see," Lau said.

Rosalie sipped a drop of water as she considered her next words. "But a gun! Here! In Bélesta! Is that really necessary? We're peaceful people here in Bélesta. You'll find no criminals here. Is that what you're doing? Are you searching for criminals?"

Lau thought for a moment before replying. "Not exactly. But we urgently need to speak to Monsieur Bernard."

"Max? What do you want with Max?"

Lau answered with a question of his own. "Do you know where he is?"

"I have no idea," Rosalie said sincerely.

"Does he go away often?"

"Away? Is he away?" Rosalie asked innocently. "Where?"

"That's what we're trying to discover, Madame…"

"Granel," Rosalie said. "I live down the street. I've lived in Bélesta all my life."

"Yes, I understand. And as I said, we're very sorry…"

"But I don't recognize you, any of you. You're not local, are you? I know the local police officers; I know everyone."

"I'm sure you do."

"Then who are you? Where are you from?"

"From Toulouse, Madame Granel."

"Toulouse? What has Toulouse to do with Bélesta?"

"All I can tell you, madame, is that we're here on a matter of national importance. And I must ask you to keep that to yourself."

"Oh, you can trust me. I never say anything to anyone. Not even my husband."

Lau forced another smile. "Now perhaps you'll permit me to escort you home?"

"But what about the cleaning?"

"I'm afraid the cleaning will have to wait this week."

"And what about Julia? Where's Julia?"

Lau reached down and gently but firmly took one of Rosalie's arms. "Allow me to help you to your feet, madame."

"But I'm still feeling a little faint."

"The air will help you," Lau said more forcefully as he hoisted the elderly woman to her feet. "You'll feel better outside."

"I can manage, thank you," Rosalie said, pulling herself free. "And there's really no need for you to come with me. I know the way."

"But I insist," Lau told her. "You're still feeling a little faint; you said so."

"I feel better now, there's no need."

"I insist, madame!"

This time Rosalie realized that there was no arguing. She sighed and walked unsteadily from the sitting room. Lau gestured to Steidle and Werner to accompany him and to the Brothers Grimm to remain where they were.

The two soldiers waited until they heard the front door shut before grinning and sitting down. "She was lucky not to get her head blown off," the more talkative of them said. "Werner's trigger-happy, he's determined to kill someone on this mission."

The other man nodded his agreement. "First the old girl was certain Werner would shoot her, then she was certain she was having a heart attack. Playing us for fools, she was. And she knows more than she's letting on."

"Hauptmann Lau knows that," the other soldier said. "That's why he's gone with her. He'll find out exactly what she knows. And if he doesn't, Steidle will."

FIFTEEN

There was an overpowering reek of garlic as the Spaniard grinned through yellowing teeth at Josette and her grandmother, Odile. At least, Josette thought it was a grin, but it could have been a sneer. The expression had already vanished and the Spaniard was now focusing on cutting another thin slice from the long, fat sausage lying on the wooden chopping board.

Josette reckoned the black sausage was probably made of wild boar, and the pungent smell that filled the room suggested it contained an almost equal amount of garlic.

The Spaniard was a familiar figure in Lavelanet. His name was Inigo, but few people knew that, and if they did, they rarely used it. To most he was simply the Spaniard, or just Spaniard. He was a small man in his mid-thirties, dark-haired, unshaven and dressed in a shirt that looked two sizes too big, and loose-fitting, baggy trousers held up by a rope belt. Inigo looked much older than his years, but his bright, darting eyes and inquisitive look hinted that he was no fool.

Inigo lived alone in a small, dilapidated cottage not far

from Odile's house close by the river. He earned his living by repairing and restoring bicycles. The tiny backyard was stacked with bits of bike: wheels, frames, handlebars, saddles, chains. Inigo was expert in mixing and matching items from unwanted bikes to make a perfectly serviceable machine.

Bits of bike somehow found their way into most rooms in the cottage. Inigo was often at work indoors, so as well as the dominant smell of garlic, there was a background aroma of old leather and grease.

"So, Inigo," Odile said, as the Spaniard deftly balanced the sliver of sausage on the blade of his razor-sharp knife, "will you help us? I'm sure our friend would be safe with you."

Inigo offered the sausage to the elderly woman, who smiled and shook her head. "Too strong for me."

The glinting blade was turned in Josette's direction, but she also quickly declined.

The small man shrugged and popped the meat into his own mouth, chewing slowly and savouring the taste as he considered Odile's question. "Well, Madame Mazet," he said after swallowing, "since I came to Lavelanet you have always been a friend to me. And you've always called me by my name."

"What else would I call you?" Odile said.

"Spaniard," Inigo said, "or the Spaniard. Do you know, I'm not even Spanish – or not what my people would call Spanish."

"You're a Basque," Odile said.

"Correct!" Inigo was delighted that his visitor remembered that he came from the region in the north of Spain where the inhabitants considered themselves a separate nation. The Spanish government believed differently. "But few bother to find out my name," Inigo continued, "and if they do, they still can't be bothered to use it. So I respect you, and I also admire you. Many people in Lavelanet admire you."

Odile was well liked in the town, but she was immune to flattery and, like her granddaughter, famed for her straight talking. "But you haven't answered my question," she said, looking Inigo in the eyes.

"I keep myself to myself these days," he said, "and I'm not looking for trouble. I've had enough of that in the past. And hiding someone from the authorities sounds like trouble to me."

"I decided to ask you partly because you keep yourself to yourself. And because I believe I can trust you."

"Thank you, Madame Mazet, that means a great deal to me, but even so, I don't think I can help."

"And what if I were to tell you that the person who needs our help says that the men who took away his wife were not gendarmes at all, but German soldiers in disguise?"

Inigo had been toying with the knife, but now his fingers tightened on the grip, his knuckles whitening. "Germans? Nazis?"

"Our friend thinks so, and we believe he's right. They are

certainly not police officers from around these parts; my son has already checked."

The Spaniard turned to Josette. "I hate Nazis, do you know that?"

"My grandmother told me," Josette answered quietly, startled by the sudden fury in Inigo's eyes.

"And did she tell you why?"

Josette shook her head.

"They killed my family in the Spanish Civil War, the fascists of General Franco and his Nazi supporters. We lived in a town called Guernica, have you heard of Guernica?"

"I'm sorry, no, I haven't."

"One day, everyone will know of Guernica. My brother and I were away fighting when the German Luftwaffe and the Italians, all Franco's allies, they came and bombed the town. No warning. They killed hundreds of defenceless civilians. Children, old people, blown to pieces. My parents, and my sister too."

He stared down at the knife clenched tightly in his hand.

Josette started to say something, but saw her grandmother give a slight shake of her head.

In the silence that followed, Josette's thoughts turned to Paul. His father had died at the hands of the Nazis, and Josette knew that Paul's constant fear was that his imprisoned mother had also been put to death.

An image of her brother, Venant, came into Josette's mind. He had been killed fighting Nazi oppression. As she glanced across at her grandmother, Josette saw Odile wipe away a tear and knew that she too had been thinking of Venant.

Eventually Inigo lifted his eyes. "Then my brother was killed in the fighting. He was just a boy. When Franco's soldiers closed in, many of us escaped across the Pyrenees into France."

This time Josette felt she could speak. "And now people are escaping the same way, but going in the opposite direction, from France into Spain."

"Escaping the Nazis," Inigo said quietly. He sighed. "You know the camp at Rivel?"

"Yes, of course," Josette said. She knew the internment camp only too well. It was the grim prison in which Jean-Pierre Dilhat had been incarcerated the previous year before escaping with the help of her father and Paul. But Jean-Pierre's freedom was fleeting. The following day he sacrificed his own life to save his friends during the failed bid to cross the mountains.

"They built that camp for us," Inigo said.

"You? But I thought…"

"Yes, now the fascists lock up French Jews there, and anyone else they don't like. But Rivel and others like it here in the south were built for escaping Spaniards during the Civil War. There was nowhere else to put us, and most of us stayed in the camps until the war was over."

"But when it ended, didn't you want to go home?"

"To what?" Inigo said. "My family dead and Franco and his fascists running the country?" He shook his head. "I can never go back. They'd hunt me down and kill me."

"I didn't know about this, Gra-mere," Josette said to her grandmother.

"Well, now you do know," Inigo said, before Odile had a chance to reply. "And perhaps now you'll understand why I hate Nazis." He turned to Odile. "Bring your friend. I'll hide him, I'll look after him like he was my brother."

Odile nodded and got to her feet. "We'll fetch him later, when there are fewer people on the streets."

"And you can tell your son, Henri, that he can depend on me too," Inigo said, leading the way to the front door. "He's been good to me, given me work when I needed it."

He paused by the door and turned back to Odile. "It's been a long time, but I'm ready to fight again."

SIXTEEN

Antoine and Rosalie Granel looked scared, and Hauptmann Kurt Lau knew, without doubt, that they were far less innocent than they made out.

Lau had a decision to make. It was clear that the elderly French couple realized now that he and his men were not regular gendarmes. But Lau hoped, and believed, that they had not guessed exactly who they were.

Since the annexation of France, many shadowy security organizations had sprung up in the Free Zone. Some were affiliated to the police, others to the Vichy government, and still more were linked directly to their German masters.

The French Deuxième Bureau had been officially dissolved the previous year, but everyone knew that many of its intelligence officers were now plying their trade on behalf of the Germans. There was the Fascist LVF, another organization cloaked in secrecy, and the Kundt Commission – German, but aided by French informers.

Just the mention of these or even more deadly organizations was enough to strike terror into the hearts of most ordinary Frenchmen and women.

Lau decided he would use fear rather than force to intimidate Antoine and Rosalie Granel. He thought he had learned as much as he could from them. And that was precious little.

Steidle and Werner had searched the house and patch of garden at the back but found nothing, exactly as Lau had expected.

But to push the Granels any more, to interrogate rather than question, would mean taking them back to the yard and that would lead to further complications; the elderly couple would probably have to die. And Lau did not want to kill them, not unless he had to.

"Madame and Monsieur Granel," he said, his voice heavy with menace, "you have refused to answer my questions truthfully, and you should know—"

"But Monsieur," Rosalie said, interrupting, "let me assure you—"

"Be quiet!" Lau yelled, and the couple shrank back into their chairs.

Lau waited, allowing the tension to grow. When he spoke again, his voice had dropped in volume, but the menace was still present. "You should know that the penalty for harbouring an enemy of France is death."

Rosalie opened her mouth to speak, but closed it again as Lau's eyes seemed to cut into her.

"You will have gathered by now," he said, "that we are not regular gendarmes. We are, in fact, part of a special

French force; you need not know the name. But I will tell you that our primary role is to hunt down and capture enemies of France. Your neighbour, Max Bernard, is one such enemy, and you are hindering his capture."

Antoine Granel reached across and took one of his wife's hands in his.

"But you are extremely fortunate," Lau continued. "We have no time to question you further, so you will be permitted to remain at liberty. For now. But make no mistake, if we return and find Max Bernard with you, or anywhere near you, or if we discover that you have discussed our visit with anyone, you will suffer the most serious consequences. Do I make myself perfectly clear?"

His eyes fixed on Antoine.

"Yes."

The steely glare switched to Rosalie.

"Oh, yes, perfectly. Sir."

Lau nodded and gestured to his men, and without another word they left the house.

Antoine and Rosalie sat side by side, breathing deeply, allowing the seconds to tick by.

And then Rosalie turned to her husband. "They're Germans."

SEVENTEEN

An engine coughed into life and Didier, astride his motorbike, nodded to Paul.

"It's them," he said, pushing down on the bike's kick-starter and feathering the engine as it started first time.

Paul climbed onto the pillion seat as Didier engaged first gear. He let out the clutch and rode slowly to the corner of the street, where he stopped. They were separated from the police Citroën by less than fifty metres, but hidden by a street and a row of houses.

They had been waiting anxiously and impatiently ever since their hurried departure from the Granels' house when Rosalie and her stern-faced escorts approached.

But there was no time now to check that the Granels were all right, because Didier and Paul were going to follow the police vehicle as it left Bélesta. If Max Bernard was right, it would cross the bridge over the Hers-Vif river and head up towards the forest.

The young men planned to follow at a safe distance. With luck they would discover where Julia Bernard was being held.

Then they would think again about their next move.

They heard the Citroën drive off and Didier pulled away, nosing the bike in the direction of the bridge.

Erich Steidle was driving the police car with Kurt Lau at his side in the passenger seat. Werner was in the back. The other two soldiers had remained at the Bernards' house, but Lau's earlier conviction that their target would return that day was quickly fading to no more than a faint hope.

The plan that had seemed so simple was unravelling. Max Bernard had disappeared into thin air, and with only five men at his disposal Lau knew he had scant hope of finding him. He needed help.

"We must bring in that oaf, Forêt," Lau said to Steidle. "He told us that Bernard never left Bélesta. But he has left, and Forêt had better come up with some ideas as to where he's gone."

Dropping a gear, Steidle eased the Citroën around a tight bend in the road that led up through the forest and waited for his commander to continue.

"Change into civilian clothes when we get back to the yard," Lau said. "The police cover is no good any more. Then go with the twins to pick up Forêt from Lavelanet. Get Forêt to come back in his car; we may need it."

Steidle's eyes remained on the road as he spoke. "Are we sure we can trust Forêt, sir?"

"Trust him? From the records I saw, he seems as genuine

as collaborators ever are. He was recruited very early by our control working out of Perpignan. Didn't need convincing, only too willing to offer his services. The Bernard lead was his first useful information."

"Nothing else, sir, before that?"

"There was something last year about a possible Resistance cell in the area, but it came to nothing when the man he suspected of leading the group was killed. A gendarme officer."

Steidle nodded and glanced into the rear view mirror. "There's a motorbike behind us, sir."

Neither Lau nor Werner turned to look back.

"And?"

"It's keeping its distance. Just about the same distance it's been since we left Bélesta."

Lau thought for a moment. "After we turn the next bend, pull over to the side of the road. We'll let him go by."

Didier was riding at a steady speed, keeping his distance, not too close and not too far behind the police vehicle.

The strategy seemed to be working.

But then, when Didier and Paul straightened the bike as they emerged from another tight bend, they saw the Citroën stopped at the roadside less than fifty metres ahead.

"You'll have to go by," Paul said into Didier's ear.

"I know," Didier replied. "Don't look at them as we pass."

But Paul did look as the motorbike passed the police vehicle, telling himself that it would be unnatural for anyone not to.

Three faces stared out at him, and the man in the front passenger seat briefly made eye contact. It wasn't a friendly look.

"I'll have to keep going," Didier said, dropping a gear as the uphill climb got steeper.

He opened the throttle and the engine whined as the bike picked up speed.

EIGHTEEN

"**N**ow what do we do?"

"I don't know."

"We should have hidden somewhere and waited for the police car to go by again," Didier said, staring back towards the forest.

"And then what? Follow them so they could stop and wait for us to pass them for a second time? Don't you think that might have given the game away?"

"But now we've lost them completely."

They had ridden all the way up through the forest road until it emerged onto the Plateau de Sault, finally stopping by a flat expanse of open land with a good view back to the treeline.

When they pulled over to the roadside, Didier told Paul that they would ride on quickly towards Espezel if the Citroën came into view. But it hadn't, and they had been waiting for at least fifteen minutes.

Paul turned towards the distant mountains. Heavy clouds were moving in quickly, threatening rain. "First time I've been up here. Didn't realize it was so bleak."

"You should see it in winter."

"I don't think I'll bother," Paul said, managing a smile as he looked back to the forest. "We haven't lost them completely. We know they're somewhere in there."

"Paul, the road through the forest is over ten kilometres long, and there are dozens of tracks running off it. We could be searching for weeks."

"Have you got a better idea?"

Didier shook his head. "They might even have gone back to Bélesta. Or somewhere else."

"No, they're in the forest."

"Probably," Didier agreed. "And if they're who we think they are, they're professionals, not amateurs like us. They'll be on their guard."

"They've got Max's wife! We have to help her."

"But not by blundering in there and getting ourselves shot. We'd better go back to Lavelanet; see what Henri suggests."

"But…"

Didier was already climbing onto his motorbike. "Come on, Paul, we can't do it all ourselves."

He was about to kick the machine into life when they heard the sound of a vehicle coming from Espezel. Looking back, they saw an old blue van approaching, smoke belching from its exhaust.

"Alain Noury," Didier said. "I know the van."

"What's he doing up here?"

"He's got a house in Espezel, belonged to his parents. He stays there sometimes even though he's got a place in Lavelanet too."

Paul laughed. "Do you know absolutely everything about everyone who lives in Lavelanet?"

"It's a small town," Didier answered, smiling. "And Alain used to work at the factory."

"Our factory?"

"Before your time, and not for very long. He can be trouble. Got a big mouth and big ideas. But he's all talk."

"And Henri sacked him?"

"No, Alain quit. There was a row over some money that went missing. No one actually accused Alain, but he walked out anyway. That's the way he was then, and he's not changed much. I saw Victor Forêt throw him out of his place yesterday."

The van was slowing.

"What does he do now?" Paul asked.

Didier shrugged. "I'm not really sure. Deals: trades, buys and sells stuff, some of it illegal, probably. I think he hoards a lot of stuff in the house at Espezel. He never seems particularly short of money."

The van came to a standstill, and Alain Noury stared out from the open window, his face hard and openly hostile. "What are you doing up here?" he said to Didier.

"Minding our own business, Alain."

"Not looking for somewhere to graze cattle, are you?"

"What?"

Alain didn't answer. His eyes, suspicious, flicked from Didier to Paul.

Sitting astride his motorbike, Didier had a good view into the van. On the passenger seat was what looked like a small bundle of rags. But there was something else too, and Didier's eyes widened in surprise as he glimpsed a short length of dull black metal poking out from beneath the rags.

Alain was about to speak as he turned back to Didier, but he spotted him looking into the vehicle and hurriedly reached across and covered the metal with the rags.

He gave the friends a contemptuous look, shoved the van's gear stick into first, stood on the accelerator and roared away. Smoke belched from the vehicle's exhaust as it rattled across the plateau.

"Grazing cattle?" Paul said as they watched the van speed across the plateau. "What was that all about?"

"I've no idea. But he had a gun on the passenger seat."

"A gun?"

Didier nodded. "A pistol. Come on, get on."

He started the machine and Paul climbed onto the pillion seat. "Why would he have a pistol?"

"I don't know," Didier said as he let out the clutch, "but he's a strange guy."

They rode across the plateau, the sky darkening by the

minute, and the first drops of rain began to fall as they entered the forest.

Didier rode carefully; the narrow, twisting road could be treacherous in wet conditions. And the rain was getting heavier. They glimpsed tracks and narrow pathways cutting through the silver fir into the gloom of the forest.

"Most of them go nowhere," Didier shouted to Paul as they rode on. "Abandoned years ago. Used to be lots of sawmills up here."

"No houses?" Paul called back.

"Not that I know of!" Didier yelled as they passed another track that was wider than most of the others. "It's not a place to live, unless you're a wild animal."

Somewhere in the distance a dog was barking, but their voices, the beat of rainfall on the road and the steady chugging of the engine combined to cover the sound.

They leaned into the next tight bend, and as the bike disappeared from view Rudi Werner stepped from behind a tree and lowered the Karabiner 98k rifle that had been aimed at Didier's head.

Hauptmann Lau was taking no chances. The moment the Citroën reached the turning for the wood yard, he had ordered Werner out of the vehicle and told him to keep watch for a full thirty minutes.

Werner followed his orders; now the thirty minutes were up. A few minutes earlier, he had fixed the rifle's sights on the driver of an old blue van as it went by.

Then it was Didier's turn.

The rain suddenly turned from heavy shower to down-pour, slamming down like hammered nails. Rumbles of thunder rolled across the sky.

Werner pulled up the collar of his jacket and shivered as water slid down his neck. He hurried up the track, the rifle's barrel pointed towards the ground to keep it dry. Perhaps, Werner thought, as he splashed through the puddles quickly forming in the mud, the kids on the bike had just been out for a spin. Or perhaps they had ridden up to the plateau on an errand, or to visit someone. Perhaps. But perhaps not.

Werner was still desperate to fire a weapon. It had been a long time.

NINETEEN

Lau's face was darker than the thunderous sky as the twins, hands tied behind their backs, were dragged into the kitchen and pushed down onto chairs.

"What the hell were you trying to do? Did you really think that two of you could get the better of *one* of my men? It would take ten of you! Twenty!"

"We don't want to see the woman hurt," Eddie said, defiantly. "We think you should set her free."

"And when did what you think start to matter?" Lau yelled. "You're being paid to do a job, and that's all. How I operate is not your concern!"

"We've made it our concern," Gilbert said, sounding as fearless as his brother. "We should never have taken your money."

"Oh, so suddenly you've developed a conscience," Lau said, his voice dropping in volume, but becoming deeper and even more threatening. "Well, it's too late for that, my friends, much too late."

Outside, the dog had resumed its ferocious barking.

The German officer frowned and turned to his radio operator, who stood next to Erich Steidle. "You did well, Berg, these idiots could have made the operation even more difficult than it is."

"I knew something was up when they came in for their meal; too many questions. When they fed their dog I watched from upstairs. I could see them plotting. I had my pistol at the ready when they made a rush for me."

"Perhaps you should have put a round into one of them," Lau said, glaring at the twins. "Or both of them!"

"I considered it, sir," Berg said, "but I decided to await your orders."

The door to the yard opened and Rudi Werner bustled in, dripping water and leaving wet, muddy footprints on the floorboards. "What's happened, sir?" he asked Lau.

"These fools tried to jump Berg." He paused before continuing slowly and deliberately. "But they already deeply regret their hasty actions, don't you, gentlemen?"

The twins remained silent.

"And they are going to cooperate fully with us from now on," Lau went on. His stare hardened. "Aren't you, gentlemen?"

This time Gilbert answered on behalf of both brothers. "You'll get no more cooperation from us."

Lau gestured to Erich Steidle, who took a step forward and cracked Gilbert across the face with the back of his right hand.

Gilbert's head jerked to the right and his cheek reddened. Blood trickled from one nostril, but he didn't make a sound as he stared defiantly at Lau.

"Which one are you?" Lau asked.

"Find out."

Lau nodded to Steidle and this time the stinging blow was delivered with much greater force. Gilbert's nose spurted crimson and more blood appeared from a cut in his top lip.

"He's Gilbert!" Eddie shouted. "And I'm Eddie. And no matter how hard you hit him, or me, we won't help you, not any more."

"Oh, yes, you'll help, Eddie," Lau said calmly. "You'll go with one of my men to Lavelanet, in your lorry. And you'll drive, as usual, so that everything looks normal and no one becomes suspicious."

"No," Eddie said.

Lau continued as though the twin had not spoken. "You'll go to Forêt's café and you'll tell him to return here, at once, in his car. You'll go, Eddie, and you won't try any tricks."

"I won't do it."

"Oh yes, you'll do it. And your brother will remain here to make sure that you do it."

"Makes no difference," Gilbert said through bloodied lips, "we'll do nothing more for you. You can't force us."

The barking outside was becoming louder, angrier, as though the dog sensed that Gilbert and Eddie were in danger.

Lau made eye contact with Werner and then glanced down at the rifle in his hands. He gestured with his head in the direction of the barking dog. Werner nodded, pulled up the collar of his coat and went outside into the rain.

"So let me repeat, so that it's perfectly clear to you," Lau said to Eddie. "You'll drive to Lavelanet with one of my men, and you'll make certain Forêt comes back here with you, but in his own car."

The dog's barking was suddenly frenzied and furious.

Eddie turned quickly to his brother as he realized what was about to happen, but before either of them could speak a single shot rang out.

And then the only sound from outside was the thud of raindrops beating against the window.

Eddie sucked in a deep breath and stared with hatred at the German officer. "You bastard," he hissed through clenched teeth.

"The next round will be for the woman," Lau told him calmly. "She is unimportant to me. And then it will be your brother. So, are you ready to drive to Lavelanet, Eddie?"

Eddie said nothing, he just nodded his head.

TWENTY

As they rode down towards Bélesta, Didier suddenly pulled the motorbike to a halt. He turned excitedly to Paul to say that he did, after all, know of people living in the forest.

"Seeing Alain Noury jogged my memory," he said. "His two cousins, Gilbert and Eddie – they're twins, they work the forest."

"And you know them?"

"Only by sight. They're identical. I think they live at the end of one of the tracks we passed."

It was something to go on. So they rode back, and as they hid the motorbike in the trees, they heard a dog barking furiously. Tyre tread marks and what looked like recent footprints were clearly visible in the wet track.

Using the trees for cover, they moved into the forest, treading lightly and staying off the track to avoid leaving their own tell-tale footprints.

Then, half a kilometre into the trees, came the sudden crack of the gun.

Paul and Didier instinctively hit the ground at the sound of the single shot that came echoing through the trees. The forest floor was spongy with compressed damp leaf litter and fir needles; the smell of rotting wood, mould and decay filled their nostrils.

The two friends lay rigid, half expecting further gunfire or shouted voices and approaching footsteps. But there was nothing: only the rain, steady and constant.

Paul raised his head just enough to turn to Didier, who was staring back at him, rain streaming down his cheek.

"Stay down," Didier whispered through a mouthful of water.

They waited as the rain pounded down, seeping through their clothes.

"I think it was a rifle, not a shotgun," Didier whispered again.

Paul nodded. "I reckon we've found them."

"Yeah, so do I."

The forest was silent now apart from the sound of the rain, which suddenly began to ease. The mountain downpours could last for just a few minutes or they could go on for hours. Fortunately for Paul and Didier, this one seemed as though it was going to be brief.

"It was the dog," Paul whispered. "Someone shot the dog."

The minutes passed and the rain stopped completely.

Birdsong returned to the woodland, but still they waited.

Shafts of weak sunlight speared through gaps in the canopy.

Finally, sensing they were safe, they nodded to each other and cautiously got to their feet. Tiny twigs and blackened leaf litter stuck to their faces, hands and clothes.

"Go on or go back?" Didier whispered, knowing full well what Paul's answer would be.

"On," Paul said, gently brushing himself down. "We have to."

Edging forward, alert for sudden danger, they moved on, following the sweep of the mud track from the cover of the trees. Even under clearing skies, the thick forest remained a dark and mysterious place.

It was a long, uncomfortable walk in cold, wet clothes, but eventually they made out the shape of a large wooden building. They paused by a pile of stacked logs and waited again, glimpsing the roof of a second, taller building standing on the far side of the first.

"That must be the Nourys' place," Didier said speculatively. "With some sort of barn behind the house."

A man's voice cut sharply through the still air and an engine rumbled into life. Paul and Didier dived behind the logs.

Peering through the trees towards the buildings, they watched a heavy lorry with a canvas covered back lumber into view from behind the house. As it passed their hiding place, they caught a quick glimpse of two men in the cab.

"The driver is one of the Noury twins," Didier breathed

to Paul. "I don't recognize the passenger."

The lorry splashed on through muddy puddles and deep ruts and disappeared around a bend in the track.

"So what now?" Didier said as the sound of the engine faded.

"We go on to make certain," Paul said with sudden authority. "We saw three men in the police car." He gestured towards the house. "If one of those was in the lorry, it means there are at least two more in the house. They wouldn't leave Max's wife on her own."

"*If* we're right about the car, and *if* they have Max's wife."

"We'll find out."

"And if they are German soldiers…"

"They are," Paul said, interrupting.

"Then they'll be armed," Didier said, "which is more than we are."

"We'll be careful, but let's find the car. Then at least we'll have something to report back to Henri. It's got to be on the far side of the house."

Didier thought for a few moments and then nodded. They crept on, moving wider to skirt around to the back of the house.

But as the yard and the rear of the house came fully into view, there was no sign of the police vehicle.

The huge barn stood face-on to the house, the two buildings forming an unconnected right angle. The barn was larger than the house and built in the same way, with over-lapping, wide planks of rough wood under a red-tiled roof. But it had no windows. The entrance was near the closest end of the front wall. There were no doors, but the space was high and wide enough for a cart or even the recently departed lorry to pass through.

"The car must be in there," Paul said quietly.

"We can't be sure," Didier answered. "And it's too risky to cross the open ground to take a closer look."

"I'll risk it," Paul said, and before Didier could argue or stop him, he was hurrying away, treading lightly over the forest leaf litter.

"Paul, wait!" Didier hissed. But it was too late; Paul had already reached the front of the tree line and was moving along its covering edge.

Short of chasing after his friend and dragging him back to safety, there was nothing Didier could do.

As he watched, Paul burst into open ground and went sprinting towards the barn. In a few brief seconds he covered thirty metres and hurtled through the wide entrance into darkness.

"Idiot," Didier breathed, relieved that Paul had at least made it to cover without being spotted.

And then the back door of the house swung open and two men emerged and strode purposefully towards the barn.

TWENTY-ONE

Paul had only seconds to react. He was peering into the police Citroën parked close to the rear wall of the barn when he heard loud laughter. It was enough to save him from immediate discovery.

By the time the two men entered the building, Paul had dashed to the back of the vehicle and was crouching down against the bumper, making himself as small as possible.

The men were speaking German, the final and absolute confirmation that Paul had been seeking. He didn't speak the language, but it was close enough to Dutch and Flemish for him to understand much of what was being said. The men had come to collect shovels or spades to bury the dog. And one of them had shot the animal: the one who had laughed as they approached the barn.

"A good shot," Paul thought he understood him to say. "He was going for me, but I hit him right between the eyes."

This time the other man laughed. "You just like to kill, Rudi."

The Germans were at the front of the car, only a couple

of metres from Paul, and they seemed in no hurry to get on with the task of burying the dog.

The vehicle sank on its suspension as one of the men leaned against the radiator grille. Then Paul heard the sound of a match striking, followed by the smell of smoke.

Paul breathed slowly, telling himself to stay calm. There was no need to panic. He was in a difficult position, but that was nothing new: he'd been in tight spots before. If he remained focused on exactly what the Germans were saying, he might well pick up snippets of important information.

As the Germans smoked their cigarettes he listened intently, not understanding everything, but getting the gist of their conversation. The mission was not going as planned. Both men wanted it over with and to get back to the north. A plane was coming for them. Soon. They were holding Max's wife, Julia; she was in the house. But they still had to find and capture Max. Then there was something about the twins, betraying the Germans, trying to free Julia and failing. That's why the dog had been killed, as a warning.

"You did well, Otto," Paul heard one of them say.

The other man laughed. "I don't only operate a radio, I had to know how to fight to get into the Brandenburgers."

Paul heard the word Brandenburgers clearly. He had no idea what it meant.

"We'd better bury that animal," the man called Otto said, and then Paul heard him grind the stub of his cigarette into the hard mud floor of the barn.

But then the other German said something else. Paul didn't grasp exactly what he said, but two words sprang out. A name. It made Paul freeze.

The conversation continued for another minute, with Paul trying desperately to comprehend the meaning of what he was hearing, or what he thought he was hearing.

Then the second man put out his cigarette with the heel of his boot. "Where did the twin say the tools were kept?"

"Hanging on the back wall."

Paul swung his head around and saw to his horror that a row of tools, including spades and shovels, hung directly behind him.

And the Germans were about to step around the car to get them.

Paul had just seconds to move and only two choices. He could make a dash for the entrance, hoping that surprise would give him the advantage as he sprinted for the forest, or he could somehow squeeze his body under the vehicle and pray that he wouldn't be heard or spotted.

He raised himself up on his haunches and discovered that his legs had gone slightly numb after crouching for so long. That didn't help, but he was going to make a dash for it: it was the better of two bad options.

He heard a footstep and went to run.

Then a loud snorting noise stopped him in his tracks.

It stopped the Germans too. "What the hell was that?"

Paul turned his head towards the source of the sound,

which had come from the inky darkness at the far end of the barn, a good twenty metres away. Close by, there were high piles of cut planks, the type the house and barn were made of. But it was difficult to see further into the gloom.

His eyes adjusted to the shadows and shapes and gradually focused on what looked like a small, self-contained structure against the far wall. It appeared to have chest-high solid walls topped with vertical wooden bars.

Something silvery moved behind the wooden bars and Paul stared.

The movement came again.

"What is it?" one of the Germans said.

And then a heavy grey horse whinnied loudly, shaking a tangled mane as it stuck its head over the half-door of the stable.

The two Germans began to laugh and went strolling towards the horse.

The horse whinnied again as the Germans approached, and Paul knew this was his chance.

Keeping his eyes on the men's backs as they neared the horse, he edged to the front of the car and tiptoed silently across the mud floor to the wide entrance. He paused, glanced out to make sure that no one else was in the yard and then sprinted into the trees.

Didier was waiting and he looked as furious as he sounded. "What the hell were you doing? You could have got yourself killed. And me!"

"I know, I'm sorry, but I had to take the risk."

Didier was generally mild tempered and rarely angry, but now he was seething. "Trying to win the war on your own again! You can't do it, Paul, it's not fair on everyone else. You didn't even stop to think."

"There wasn't time, and anyway, what was there to think about?"

"Footprints for a start, when you ran across the yard."

Paul glanced back towards the yard. "It's still wet and churned up, my footprints don't show."

"And what about inside the barn? Wet footprints on dry mud? It's a complete giveaway."

"But it's so dark in there, they'd never see footprints."

Didier took a deep breath, the anger in his face starting to fade. "You got lucky. This time."

"Look, I'm sorry, Didier, you're right; I should have stopped to think. But I know what's going on now, they were talking and I could understand most of what they said."

"And?"

"They've got Max's wife in the house, and the Noury twins have been working for them. But not any more – they tried to free Julia and that's why the Germans killed their dog."

"How many are there?"

"I'm not sure. Those two, an officer in the house, the one who went in the lorry, and we know they left two more at

Max's house, that's six. Maybe there are more. But there's something else…"

Didier suddenly raised one finger to his lips and Paul fell silent. He looked back and saw the two Germans, both carrying a shovel, striding away from the barn. They crossed the yard and went around to the front of the house.

"Something else?" Didier whispered, when he was certain the Germans were out of earshot.

Paul nodded. "The person who helped the Germans organize this whole operation is Victor Forêt."

"Forêt?" Didier said, stunned. "Victor Forêt? From Lavelanet? He's helping … he's a collaborator?"

"They've gone for him now," Paul said. "In the lorry we saw leaving. Forêt's been providing them with information about Max Bernard. And they're banking on him leading them to him again."

TWENTY-TWO

Victor Forêt stared nervously out through the café window, across the terrace and the small square to the lorry parked on the far side.

He couldn't see the face of the German sitting in the cab but he knew the man was staring in his direction. Silently commanding him to obey orders.

Victor was behind the bar and Eddie Noury was on the other side. Both looked panicked at the way events were panning out.

"You got us into this, Victor," Eddie said. "You have to get us out."

"Quiet!" Victor said. He seemed short of breath and his face was crimson. "You want everyone to hear?"

The café was hardly packed: the only customers were two elderly men nursing half-full glasses of beer at a table close to the front.

"I can't just close the place," Victor whispered, glancing towards the two beer-drinkers. "People will become suspicious." Beads of sweat stood out on his brow.

"You have to come with me, now," Eddie said, louder than he had intended.

One of the men at the front looked towards them, but went back to his beer without making a comment.

"They've threatened to kill Gilbert," Eddie hissed. "And the woman."

Victor wiped the back of one hand across his sweaty brow. "Why did you have to interfere? You should have kept your noses out."

"But we didn't! And it's too late to change that now. We have to do what they say." Eddie glanced out towards the lorry. "And we can't keep him waiting, he said to be quick."

Victor took another look through the window. "And why do they want my car?"

"Just do as they say, Victor," Eddie hissed. "Now!"

The café owner sighed heavily and nodded towards the staircase at the back of the long bar. "I'll have to get Celine down. She won't like it; she's resting. Give me five minutes."

Victor was married, but not to Celine who was upstairs in the flat above the café. Victor's wife, Christine, had suddenly departed Lavelanet one summer night several years earlier. She told a friend that she was leaving because Victor bored her and bullied her and sometimes, when he was drunk, beat her. The drunkenness and the beatings were increasing in frequency and Christine had finally had enough. She disappeared that night and had never been seen or heard of since.

Victor waited a couple of years before moving in her replacement. But Celine was very different to her predecessor. She was a big woman, muscular and strong. Celine was immune to Victor's boring conversation and she ignored his bullying ways and gave as good as she got in a fight. Celine would stand up to any man, and frequently did when there was trouble in the bar, and Victor had quickly learned not to tangle with her, even when he was drunk.

A few minutes after trudging up the stairs, Victor returned to the bar, with Celine plodding down behind him.

She was taller than Victor, and broader, and she looked ferocious. "How long will you be?" she growled. "I'm not standing here on my own all night."

"I don't know," Victor grunted, equally sourly. "I'll be back when I'm back."

They glared at each other, then Victor gestured for Eddie to follow him from the café.

There was no one on the terrace; the earlier rain had soaked the tables and chairs and driven people indoors. And as evening approached the temperature was dropping. It was too cold for the terrace now.

Victor mumbled that he would meet the lorry at his lock-up garage a few streets away. As Eddie crossed the square and climbed into the cab, Victor plodded away, up a narrow lane to one side of the café. The lane was not wide enough for the lorry; Eddie would have to take a different route, but he knew the way.

The lorry pulled away, and as it turned the corner someone else emerged from behind one of the trees on the square and walked across to the lane.

Alain Noury had a score to settle with the café owner. He'd been waiting and wondering whether or not he should go inside. He really wanted to get Victor on his own. There was a loaded pistol in his pocket. Alain intended to give the café owner the fright of his life, along with a warning that if he messed with him again he'd end up with a bullet in his head. That was the plan. Then Victor had emerged from the café, but with one of his cousins in tow. He didn't know which of his cousins – he could never tell from a distance – but he'd driven off now, anyway.

Alain was ready to grab his opportunity. As he entered the lane, he saw Victor up ahead and watched him turn left. Alain had warned him he'd be sorry. Victor had to learn his lesson, like others before him had.

Everyone needed to know that you didn't mess with Alain Noury.

Victor's temper was close to boiling point by the time he reached his lock-up garage. The uphill walk was hardly strenuous, but it had left him panting. Why did they want him to go to them in his own car? Victor's car was the only thing that was precious to him.

He kept the highly polished black Peugeot 402 in immaculate condition. Only two nights earlier, he'd eased it extra cautiously along that long, bumpy track to the wood yard. It had left the vehicle mud-spattered and in need of a thorough cleaning, which had taken an hour. It would be even worse this time, after the rain. And the rutted track was murder on any car's suspension.

Victor was always brave when he was alone. He told himself that he wasn't going to ferry the Germans around in his car. He wasn't a chauffeur or a taxi driver and he wouldn't be at their beck and call.

He would go to the yard, answer their questions and offer what advice he could, but that was it. He wasn't being paid enough to fight their war for them.

There was no one around; the quiet back street was deserted. Eddie's lorry had not yet arrived.

Victor unlocked the double doors and slipped the key into a pocket. He pulled open one door and then the other. As he stepped into the darkness of the garage, he thought he heard someone running.

Then the lorry turned into the road.

Victor unlocked the car and slid into the driver's seat. The vehicle started first time, as always, and he carefully eased the Peugeot from the garage onto the road. He stopped the car, pulled on the handbrake and switched off the engine.

In the lorry's cab, Erich Steidle rolled his eyes and sighed as he watched Victor haul himself from the Peugeot. "What's he doing now?" he said to Eddie.

"I think he's going to lock the garage."

"But why? It's empty now."

"Victor's a cautious man."

They watched as the café owner methodically closed the two doors. He was rooting in his pockets for the key to the lock when Steidle swore and thumped a clenched fist down on the dashboard. "Let's go. He knows the way, he can catch us up."

Eddie shrugged, shoved the lorry into gear and drove away.

His cousin, Alain Noury, had turned on his heels and run for cover when he heard the lorry approaching. He didn't want to be seen by anyone, and particularly not by one of his cousins. He'd almost reached Victor when the lorry turned up.

What was going on? What connection was there between the twins and Victor Forêt? As far as Alain knew, they didn't use his café very often, and Gilbert hadn't mentioned their seeing Victor when they'd met on the plateau the previous day. He'd said they were busy in the yard. And Alain had just spotted a stranger sitting in the cab with the twin. Another stranger. What was going on?

Skulking around a corner, Alain was trying to make sense of what he'd seen. He heard the lorry move off again and waited. Was it really leaving this time, or just moving further down the street?

Alain was confused, and he became edgy and unpredictable when he was confused.

He listened as the rumble of the lorry's diesel engine faded. Now, at last, Alain had his chance.

He slipped his hand into his jacket pocket and his fingers gripped the cold metal. Victor was going to be very sorry for what he'd done. He had to learn. Alain took a step forward. He heard the Peugeot's engine start. He turned the corner just as the shiny black vehicle pulled away.

Another opportunity was lost.

Victor was in no hurry; he would make the Germans wait. Always a careful driver, he never drove particularly fast, and certainly never drove dangerously.

The light was beginning to fade, so Victor switched on the Peugeot's head lamps as he manoeuvred the car through the narrow backstreets and on towards the river.

The lorry had disappeared, but it was a cumbersome and slow vehicle. Even driving at his usual leisurely pace, Victor knew he would catch it up before he reached the lines of plane trees on the road leading into Bélesta. From there he would follow it to the forest.

There was no one about – it was nearing the hour when most people would be at home having dinner – but turning a corner, Victor caught a glimpse of three people entering the road he had just left. Two women and a man.

He drove on for a hundred metres or so, then jammed on the brakes, bringing the Peugeot to a skidding halt.

It was him! Max Bernard! He had the collar of his coat

pulled up, but there was no hiding that lanky frame and wild shock of hair. It was him, with the Mazet girl and her grandmother. Victor was absolutely certain. Max Bernard was here in Lavelanet!

He stared up the deserted street. The lorry was long gone. Why hadn't they waited? It could have been all over, there and then. Finished. And Victor would have been the hero. And paid, too.

But maybe he still could be. He would follow Bernard and the others, see where they went, then report back to the Germans. The road was tight; it would be easier to drive to the end, turn around and drive back.

He put the car into first and pulled away, driving much faster than usual. Just as he reached the end of the street, a man on a bicycle came suddenly around the corner, turning too wide. Victor braked, his heart in his mouth, as the bike lurched towards the car. He wrenched on the steering wheel and the Peugeot swerved. The bicycle wobbled and came to a standstill.

The rider was an elderly man. Victor knew him slightly. He glared into the car. "What d'you think you're doing, going so fast? Are you in a race? You could kill someone driving like that!"

"You were too far out in the road!" Victor yelled back. "You should watch where you're going, silly old fool!"

"Don't you shout at me, Victor Forêt! I suppose you're drunk on your own wine again! And I'll ride my bicycle how I like, I've lived in this road all my life."

"Well, it's a miracle you've lived so long, then! Now get out of my way!"

Swearing under his breath, Victor drove on. He turned the corner, stopped, reversed, stopped again and drove back into the road he had just left. The man on the bicycle shook a fist as the car passed, and Victor mouthed another curse.

He'd lost time, but hopefully he would see Bernard and the others when he turned the next corner.

He didn't. They were nowhere to be seen.

Victor drove slowly on, peering into lighted windows on both sides of the road.

He passed a turning on his right. Nothing. He reached a junction with roads going both left and right. Nothing.

Victor swore loudly. He'd lost them.

TWENTY-THREE

Odile Mazet had a way of making most people feel at ease. Inigo and Max were total strangers and from different worlds, but within minutes of being introduced they were talking comfortably.

Max was still frantic with worry about his wife and desperate for news of her, but Inigo had brought out a bottle of some sort of spirit, filled two small glasses and, after a toast to freedom, began telling his new guest about his own battles against fascism.

Odile and Josette refused the offer of a drink. They listened politely as Inigo spoke, but Josette's thoughts were elsewhere. She was worried, too – about Paul and Didier. They'd been gone since early morning, leaving for Bélesta with Max's friend, Antoine Granel, but now it was evening and they had not returned, and no word had come through.

They couldn't telephone; Max had said there was no phone at either his or Antoine's house. But they couldn't possibly still be with Antoine, they must have gone somewhere else. But where? And why?

It was frustrating not knowing. And Josette wasn't just worried; she was also highly put out that she wasn't involved in the action. She didn't want to babysit Max; she wanted to be out there on the front line, doing her bit. But when Paul and Didier decided to go to Bélesta that morning, they had just assumed that it would be they who went, and not Josette.

She hadn't argued at the time but she'd been getting more and more angry about it all day. It was always the same, just because she was a girl.

She was thinking that she would make her feelings perfectly clear to both Paul and Didier when they did get back, when there was an urgent knocking at the front door. Everyone in the room tensed.

Inigo was the first to react. "Out the back," he said to Max. "In the privy. Lock yourself in and stay quiet."

Max glanced anxiously at Odile, who nodded. Silently the scientist got to his feet and went out the back door to the small yard.

Inigo, Odile and Josette watched through the window and saw him go into the tiny wooden lavatory building.

The knocking on the front door resumed. Odile picked up the glass that Max had been drinking from and placed it on the table in front of her.

Inigo was on his feet. He opened the door of a tall, upright cabinet and pulled out a slim, sharp-bladed knife, which he slipped into the back of his belt.

"It might not come to it, but just in case," he said to Odile. "I swore years ago that no fascist would ever take me. I meant it then and I mean it now. But I'm sorry you two are here."

Odile and Josette said nothing, but as Inigo went through to the room leading to the front door, Odile took her granddaughter's hand and held it tightly.

They heard the door swing open, and then Inigo's voice. "Oh, it's you! Come in, come in."

Josette's heart was pounding in her chest. Her father walked into the room.

"Papa!" she said almost angrily. "You terrified us!"

Henri looked bewildered. "I just knocked on the door. What was I meant to do? And where's Max?"

Josette and Odile turned to look through the rear window at the tiny outside lavatory. Then they turned back and looked at each other. And for the first time that day, they laughed.

"I was thinking about what Paul said this morning," Henri said when Max had returned to the room. "And he was right; if Antoine Granel has heard rumours about me running a Resistance group here in Lavelanet, then others have almost certainly heard them, too."

Odile slowly nodded her head. "And with new enemies nearby, that becomes even more dangerous."

"Exactly. That's why I thought it best to meet here, rather than at home or the factory." He turned at Inigo.

"That is, if you don't mind, of course."

"I'm honoured, Henri," the Spaniard said, refilling his glass to the brim and downing it in one go.

Josette couldn't stop herself from thinking that if Inigo kept drinking at that pace he wouldn't be much use if it came to a fight. But she stopped herself from mentioning it.

"What about Paul and Didier," she asked her father, "any word from them?"

Henri shook his head. "From them, no."

"Then what do we do?" Max asked urgently. "We can't sit here doing nothing, those people have my wife!"

"We can only wait," Henri replied. "Paul and Didier have been gone for most of the day; we must hope they've discovered something. I've left instructions with my wife for them to come here as soon as they get back."

"You said you hadn't heard from them," Odile said to her son. "Does that mean you've heard from someone else?"

"Yes, I have. From London; news about *Eagle*."

"Eagle?" Max said, looking confused. "What is *Eagle*?"

"It's … it's the codename for … for another operation we are involved in." Belatedly, Henri had realized that he shouldn't have mentioned *Eagle* in front of Max or Inigo, or, come to that, his mother. It was information they didn't need to know.

Nevertheless, Inigo was impressed. "Wonderful," he said, thumping down a flattened palm on the table. He refilled his glass again and lifted it in a toast. "Death to all fascists!"

TWENTY-FOUR

At last Victor Forêt was receiving the respect he deserved. He felt better, much less tense, and the tightness gripping his chest for the past couple of days was easing at last.

He had reported his sighting of Max Bernard to the German officer, who thanked him generously and complimented him on his observational skills. If the German was at all angry or even frustrated that Victor had spotted Bernard and then lost him again within seconds, he didn't show it. And when Victor announced that he had even more vital information, Lau smiled indulgently. "Please continue," he said.

"The old woman and the girl I saw with Bernard, they are family to Henri Mazet, his mother and his daughter."

"And?"

Victor sat back in his chair and rested the interlocked fingers of his hands on his bulging beer gut. He was more confident now. "Last year I suspected that Henri Mazet was part of the Resistance group I thought was operating in

Lavelanet. I sent in my report; perhaps you saw it?"

Lau nodded.

"You may remember that I also suspected a gendarme officer, Gaston Rouzard, of being part of the group."

"Yes, I read that."

"But then Rouzard was killed and the rumours of a Resistance group faded away. There wasn't much to report on after that, people here seemed to have lost their appetite for resistance."

"Remind me of how this Rouzard died?"

"He was shot. No one was ever charged with the crime and there were no suspects. Gaston was a policeman and sometimes policemen make enemies. But seeing Max Bernard with the Mazet women today made me think that I was right after all about Henri Mazet. He must be Resistance, Bernard knew that and went to him for help. It seems likely, don't you think?" Victor smiled his most ingratiating smile and waited while Lau considered his theory.

"You know where Henri Mazet lives?"

"Yes, it's a big house close to the edge of town. Stands on its own; all very grand. He owns the biggest textile factory in Lavelanet, too. Plenty of money."

"And his mother, does she live with him?"

"No, she has a house by the river. I know the house – not the street name or the number, but I could show you the place. When I was driving here I realized that Bernard must be in hiding there."

Lau beckoned to his radio operator, Otto Berg. "Make contact with headquarters and tell them I am confident we will capture our target tomorrow. Set a time as soon as possible for the pick-up."

"Yes, sir."

Berg left the room and Lau turned to his second-in-command, Erich Steidle. "Bernard won't return to Bélesta, so it's pointless watching his house any more. Go and fetch the others – we'll need them tomorrow. Use our friend Monsieur Forêt's car."

"My car!" Victor said looking horrified. "But—"

"Unless you have any objections, monsieur," Lau said, his voice suddenly much less cordial.

Victor's newfound confidence swiftly drained away. "No … not objections … not exactly." He looked at Steidle. "But you will take care of the car, won't you?"

Steidle grinned. "I'll treat it as though it were my own." He held out one hand, palm upwards. "Keys?"

Reluctantly, Victor dug into a pocket and brought out the keys to his car. Steidle took them, nodded and left without another word.

As the door closed, Lau smiled at Victor. "You'll be staying here with us tonight."

"What!"

"You told me you can show us the way to the old woman's house. You'll do exactly that first thing in the morning."

"But ... but I can't stay here. I have customers ... my café..."

"Monsieur Forêt, I have much to do this evening, so please don't waste my time. You'll go with two of my men to the woman's house, and if, as you predict, Bernard is hiding there, they'll bring him back here. My own team will target his other possible hiding place. This time Max Bernard will not escape us." He smiled at Victor. "Then your part of the operation will be finished and you can return to your café in your precious car."

The tension gripping Victor's chest had returned. His bottom lip dropped; he was short of breath. He stared, mouth gaping.

"Close your mouth, Monsieur Forêt," Lau said. "You look like a fish."

Victor snapped his mouth shut.

"Of course, that leaves me the twins to deal with," Lau continued, to himself more than to Victor. "I would be justified in shooting them both after the way they betrayed us."

The twins were locked in a room upstairs, along with Julia Bernard.

Victor's main concern, as always, was for himself. "But if you shoot them, that would mean all sorts of complications later," he managed to gasp. "How would it be explained? They've been seen with me, there would be questions. My cover could be compromised."

"I don't intend to shoot them," Lau said curtly. "We'll

need their lorry in the operation tomorrow, and when we leave here for good they'll do exactly as they were originally meant to do: provide the torches for our plane when it lands. If they cooperate, with no further stupidity or heroic actions, they'll live."

The words were spoken casually, but the threat was there, as it always was with Hauptmann Kurt Lau.

As Victor nodded his head vigorously, the radio operator returned to the room.

"Yes?" Lau said.

"Weather report for tomorrow is good, sir: a full moon, clear sky. After that it's more uncertain for several days. So pick-up is set for tomorrow, sir, at around midnight."

Lau smiled. "Good. We'll be ready."

TWENTY-FIVE

The pistol felt as though it was burning a hole in Alain Noury's pocket.

A lot of old weapons had made their way across the Pyrenees during the Spanish Civil War. Spanish weapons, German, Russian, American, even ancient Mexican rifles had been carried across the mountains with the fleeing Republicans.

Some had been given away, others sold, exchanged for food, stolen, or ferreted away to be sold at a future date.

That was how Alain Noury had come into possession of his "Spanish Colt" pistol. It was called the Spanish Colt because it was an exact replica of the US army issue Colt 45, but smaller and 9mm. The pistol, with a supply of ammunition, had become his for just a few francs a couple of years earlier.

And having fetched it from its usual hiding place at the house in Espezel, Alain felt now that at the very least it had to be brandished.

He was sitting in his van, across the square from the café,

waiting for Victor Forêt to return.

Night had fallen and Alain was cold and fed up. He wanted to know what had happened to Victor, but was getting tired of waiting.

He looked over to the café for what was probably the twentieth time, then, deciding to take a chance, climbed out of the van and strode quickly across the square.

The doorbell jangled as he pushed open the café door. Every head turned in his direction. Not a lot happened in Forêt's bar at night: a new arrival was something to break the boredom.

Alain felt uneasy as he stepped inside, not knowing if Victor had told Celine that he'd thrown him out of the café and banned him from coming back. If Celine ordered Alain out, he would go without an argument. He didn't want to get into a fight with Celine. More importantly, he didn't want to be known as someone who had been beaten in a fight with her.

But as he stepped up to the bar, it seemed as though his fears were unfounded. Celine managed a grudging nod. It wasn't exactly a warm welcome, but it was as good as it got with Celine.

"A beer, please," Alain said, a little tentatively.

Celine drew the beer, thudded the glass onto the bar top and picked up the few coins Alain had placed there. She said nothing; giving customer satisfaction was not Celine's way.

Relaxing a little, Alain sipped his beer and glanced around the room at the half a dozen men seated at tables. He recognized them all, but no one showed any interest in starting a conversation. That suited Alain: he was there for information, not a friendly chat.

It was hardly warmer inside the café than it had been out in the van. In the open stove, a single log appeared to be losing the battle to stay alight. More logs were stacked to one side, but none of the customers had been brave enough yet to lift one from the pile and slide it into the stove: if Celine wanted the place warmer, she would do it herself.

"Where's Victor tonight?" Alain asked Celine, who had propped her burly frame onto a wooden stool and was sawing at her pink-painted fingernails with a metal file.

She scowled, but didn't look up as she continued with her work. "You tell me. Went out hours ago and left me here minding the place. Like a servant! I'll kill him when he gets back!"

Alain smiled and took another sip of beer, but then Celine stopped sawing her nails and glared at him. "It was your cousin he went with, one of those twins from the forest. What are they are up to? Where've they gone, eh?"

"No idea," Alain said. "Didn't Victor tell you?"

"I wouldn't be asking you if he'd told me, would I?" Celine growled. She went back to her nails and then sighed loudly as a customer approached the bar. Reluctantly she hauled herself off the stool to serve him.

Alain drained his beer. There was no point in staying any longer; he'd learned as much as he was going to, and if Victor did turn up, there would be trouble.

"Thanks," he said. Celine didn't bother to reply.

Nodding to a couple of the men, he left and returned quickly to his van. But then Alain saw two figures approaching the café. They didn't go in, but stopped at the front of the terrace. They appeared to be looking inside.

Alain waited and watched. He couldn't make out who they were. The square was dimly lit and the lights from the café only silhouetted the figures. After a few moments they turned and walked away.

Quietly, Alain stepped from the van and followed them, slipping his hand into his jacket pocket and curling his fingers around the pistol as he walked.

They went into the same narrow side street that Victor had taken earlier. Alain followed again, keeping his distance as before. The street was unlit, but thin strands of dull yellow light spilled from the gaps in closed shutters.

Alain could hear footsteps and low, muttered voices. Then the footsteps stopped.

Alain stopped too. He backed into the shadows of a porch.

An engine started; seconds later a motorbike passed by. Alain caught a glimpse of Didier Brunet and his friend Paul.

Them again. First on the plateau and now here. It couldn't be a coincidence. They were up to something.

Alain's grip on the pistol tightened. He already had a score to settle with those two, along with Henri Mazet and his daughter, Josette. Everything that had happened the previous year was their fault. It was all down to them.

Alain had been part of a lucrative and enterprising business based on robbery and murder. The victims were wealthy northerners, usually Jews, fleeing the Nazis and desperate to cross the Pyrenees to Spain and freedom. Alain, Gaston and Yvette would deliver them into the hands of their contacts, a group of Andorran mountain men.

Yvette was related to one of the Andorrans who would lead their hapless, disorientated and frightened victims part way across the mountains and then kill them, stealing their valuables and cash before disposing of their bodies.

It was going well and they were all making a small fortune. Gaston had grand ideas about taking over the local Resistance movement and using some of his cash to spread misinformation and disrupt their actions. Gaston had been old-fashioned. He wanted stability and order, and as far as he was concerned, that meant Marshal Petain and the Vichy government staying in power.

Alain and Yvette had no such ideals. They just wanted the money, and more of it.

Then Henri Mazet and the others ruined everything by killing the Andorrans and discovering Yvette and Gaston's involvement in the scheme. Alain would have been next, which was why he had had to kill Yvette and Gaston, to stop them from giving him away. He hadn't wanted to do it – it was a shame, a great pity – but there really was no alternative.

But ever since then, he had planned his revenge on Mazet and the others. It looked now as though the time for that revenge was fast approaching.

Alain sighed as he walked back to his van, the metal of the Spanish Colt warm in his hand.

He'd fetched the pistol from its hiding place merely to frighten Victor, but suddenly that didn't seem quite enough any more. Alain had a strong feeling that one way or another the pistol would kill again before very long.

TWENTY-SIX

Five faces were turned in Henri's direction, waiting for his guidance and words of wisdom, but Henri had no idea what he should say next. He had a lot on his mind and was rhythmically smoothing down the bristles of his moustache with the index finger of his right hand, as he often did when worried.

The five of them were squeezed into the back room at Inigo's little house, seated at a rickety wooden table littered with bottles, glasses, empty coffee cups and plates bearing the remnants of a hastily assembled meal.

Paul and Didier had returned tired and hungry. As they began to tell their story, Inigo fetched bread, cheese and more of his foul-smelling garlic-stuffed sausage.

The two friends spoke as they ate, explaining what had happened at Bélesta and in the forest. Paul told of how he had managed to overhear the information about Julia, the Germans, the twins and Victor Forêt, ommitting to mention the dangerous situation in the barn.

Max was elated that his wife had been located. She was

still a prisoner, yes, but at least now they knew exactly where she was being held.

And the revelation that Victor Forêt was collaborating with the enemy was no shock at all to Josette. "I *told* you I didn't trust that man, didn't I!" she exclaimed excitedly to Didier.

"And I told you too," Josette said to Paul. "Remember when you first arrived here, I said I was suspicious of Victor, didn't I?"

Josette turned her attention to her father. "He's the traitor, and he killed Yvette, and Gaston Rouzard too."

"That isn't necessarily the case, Josette."

"But it must be; it's obvious."

"No," Henri said firmly, "it's not obvious. It's possible, that's all. Our main focus must be on what we know for certain."

"We went to the café earlier," Didier said. "We know for certain that Victor wasn't there."

"So he's with the Germans," Josette said quickly. "He has to be."

"No, he *may* be with the Germans, Josette," Henri corrected.

Josette sighed loudly, exasperation written all over her face.

"I know we can't act purely on wild guesses, Henri," Paul said, "but we have to consider all possibilities now, for our own safety."

"Yes, I agree."

"Then we have to accept that Victor Forêt may well know about our Resistance group and that he has told the Germans about us. It was known in Bélesta, which means it's even more likely to be known here in Lavelanet."

Didier nodded his agreement. "So it's possible that the Germans suspect Max has come to you for help."

"Highly possible, yes, which means we must take great care."

Josette was impatient to get on. "We will take care, of course, but what do we do next, Papa?"

Henri wasn't in the least bit surprised that the direct question about a tactical plan had come from his daughter. His mother, Odile, had left earlier, and Henri had very briefly attempted to convince Josette that she should go too.

Josette's response was exactly what Henri had anticipated. "No, Papa, I'm not going! I will not be excluded any more! I'm part of this, like Paul, like Didier and like you!"

She was right. Henri knew, much as he wanted to, that he could not exclude Josette from the operation. And even if he did, she'd force her way in somehow and that would only increase the danger for them all.

Now Paul, Didier, Josette, Max and Inigo were staring at Henri, waiting to hear his plan, but he'd been wracking his brains and had nothing concrete to offer.

The previous year, when setting up the Resistance cell, he'd given himself the code name Reynard for secrecy when in radio communications with other groups. He'd chosen Reynard because an old business friend often called him a wily old customer in business deals, cunning like a fox, and always ready with a plan or idea.

But now Henri had no ideas at all. He took a breath, thinking furiously but playing for time. "There are at least six Germans," he said at last. "We know that from Paul and Didier. We also know they are trained soldiers and fully armed. We can't possibly outfight them, so—"

"We can try!" Josette interrupted.

"Josette!" Didier said impatiently. "Listen to your father."

Josette glared at Didier but stayed silent.

"Our only objective," Henri continued, trying to figure out tactics as he talked the situation through, "is to free Max's wife." He spoke softly. "We can't concern ourselves with fighting the Germans – or dealing with Victor Forêt, or for the moment, with anything else – we just have to free Julia. So…" Henri hesitated, and everyone around the table leaned forward slightly in their chair.

"Yes, Papa?" Josette said, in little more than a whisper.

"So…"

Paul and Didier exchanged a look.

"So … I'm open to suggestions on how we proceed from here."

There was a collective sigh of disappointment. For a few moments no one spoke.

"Henri's right," Paul said at last. "We can't outfight the Germans." He remembered what Didier had said to him earlier as he continued. "And we shouldn't take *unnecessary* risks; we have to think of the safety of us all."

"So what do we do?" Max Bernard asked urgently. "We must free my wife."

"And we will," Paul replied. He glanced at Didier. "And we will have to take risks – *necessary* risks. But as we can't outfight the enemy, we'll have to use tactics and cunning." He looked at Henri. "Eh, Reynard?"

"What are you getting at, Paul?" Didier asked. "What tactics?"

Henri spoke up before Paul could answer. "Look, there's something else you need to know, Paul."

"About what?"

"It's *Eagle*," Henri said. "It's on."

"Oh," Paul breathed. In the excitement and tension of the day, *Eagle* had completely slipped from his mind. "When?"

Henri hesitated. After his earlier mistake he'd said nothing more in front of Max and Inigo about the operation. But with events moving so swiftly and *Eagle* imminent, there seemed little point in holding back the information from anyone in the room. "Tomorrow."

"What!"

"Tomorrow night."

"No, not tomorrow, it can't be then. They'll have to put it back for a few days."

Henri shook his head. "That's impossible, you know that."

"But I'm not ready to go."

"Paul, do you realize how much planning has gone into this operation? The British Government, their secret forces, the Royal Navy – they're all involved, as well as our contacts in Portugal and Spain. And our Resistance friends from nearby."

"Nearby?"

"Limoux and Puivert. The movement is growing, Paul, and these people are coming to help you."

Inigo raised his bushy eyebrows and his eyes widened as he looked at Paul. "You must be a very important person."

"We have to tell them I've changed my mind, Henri," Paul said. "I don't want to go."

"It's too late for that, Paul. You made your decision, you have to stick to it."

"Then just ask them to give me a few more days."

"I told you, that's impossible. The weather reports say tomorrow night will be clear with very light winds; perfect for a small plane to land. After that, the weather is predicted to turn bad, possibly for a week or more; with rain and low cloud a plane couldn't land. So it must be tomorrow night."

The room fell silent. Everyone's eyes were on Paul. He thought rapidly before speaking again. "Then our only chance to rescue Julia is tomorrow morning."

"What!" Henri and Max said together.

"Why, Paul?" Didier said. "Why tomorrow?"

"Because if a plane is coming for me tomorrow night, then another has to be coming for the Germans."

"How can you be so sure?"

"I heard them say it was soon. They'll have had the weather reports too; they'll know their only chance of getting out is tomorrow. But they have to find Max first, which means they have to go searching for him. And while they're away from the wood yard, we'll go in and snatch Julia."

Everyone stopped to consider. Paul's reasoning made sense and was even the beginning of a plan of action.

"You make it sound easy," Didier said eventually.

"I know it won't be easy, but it's our only chance."

"But they're not fools; they won't leave Julia completely unguarded."

"No, but a single guard, or even two, will be a lot easier to fight than six heavily armed Germans."

"We agreed before that we couldn't fight them."

"All right, we don't fight them, we draw the guards from the house by creating some sort of diversion. You still have your shotgun, don't you?"

"Yes, of course."

"We can make a noise with that."

Inigo had been listening intently, looking from one face to another. "If you want to create a diversion, and a big noise, I can do a lot better than a shotgun."

"How?" Paul asked.

"In my war, in Spain, we had to make many of our own weapons. I became an expert in home-made grenades and petrol bombs. I'll make a few of those." He laughed. "They'll give you your diversion."

Paul smiled. "Excellent."

Didier turned to Henri. "If Paul's right, and the Germans do go searching for Max tomorrow, we also have to consider where they'll go."

Henri sighed wearily. He was acutely aware that the younger members of his group were thinking much more quickly and tactically than him.

"And where do you think they'll go, Didier?"

"They'll start with you."

"Me?"

"Yes, you and those close to you. If Victor has told them you lead the Resistance group here, then you're their obvious starting point. Get you and maybe they'll get Max. That will be their thinking."

"Yes, but this is still just speculation."

"But I think he's right," Paul said quickly. "And even if he's not, they have to go looking for Max tomorrow; it's their last chance. So we have to act while we can. We'll need vehicles; your bike, Didier, and your car, Henri."

Henri sighed. "Paul, even if you are right about this…"

"He is right, Papa," Josette said urgently.

"*Probably* right," Henri agreed. "But I should forbid you to be part of the operation, Paul, for the sake of the information you have for the Allies."

"You need me, Henri."

"It's true," Josette said, "we do need him."

"We're too few as it is," Didier agreed.

Henri considered for a long moment before speaking. "Very well. But a Lysander light aircraft will touch down on the landing strip outside Puivert at ten minutes to midnight tomorrow night. When it takes off again you must be on it, Paul."

TWENTY-SEVEN
Day Four

It was one a.m. Paul checked his watch as a church clock in the centre of town struck the hour. He was alone, writing a letter, trying to get down everything that needed to be said.

He could hear the faint murmur of voices downstairs. Paul knew he should be trying to sleep, but the letter had to be written, and besides, he was wide awake, buzzing, an electric energy pulsing through his veins at the thought of what was to come during the next few hours.

They were going into danger, into the unknown. Anything might happen: there was a chance he might not survive, and it was not just a remote chance. The letter had to be written.

Paul was agonizing over every word, trying to ensure that what he wrote was exactly right. And as he wrote, his thoughts kept returning to his parents and his previous life in Antwerp, seeing his father gunned down on the dockside and then hearing that his mother had been arrested and dragged away by the Germans. Where was she now? Was she even alive?

He stopped writing and stared at the wall as he guiltily realized he had not once thought about his parents during the previous twenty-four hours.

It was a shocking realization.

Until then he had thought about them every day, first thing in the morning when he woke up and last thing at night as he tried to go to sleep. And they were always in his dreams: his dark, disturbing dreams.

The constant pain of losing his parents had eased a little over the months. But it was still there, nagging away, and it would always be there.

Paul had vowed that he would one day return to Antwerp to hunt down the person who had betrayed his parents. To keep that vow he had to survive.

But for now all those thoughts had to be put to the back of his mind. In a few hours he was going into action, which was what he had wanted for so long. And this time they were going on the offensive instead of fighting a merely defensive battle.

Paul could hear his heart thudding in his chest. Was it always like this before action, this sensation of feeling sick in the pit of the stomach but at the same time dizzy with anticipation and desperate to get the job done?

Inigo had spoken earlier about his experiences fighting on the front line during the Spanish Civil War. He said he'd been afraid every time, because only a fool was never scared.

"Only a fool was never scared." The words had stuck in

Paul's mind and they came back to him now.

He returned to his letter, making certain everything was in order just in case the worst did happen.

But then he stopped suddenly. What if his prediction was wrong? What if the Germans didn't come searching for Max tomorrow and just sat tight at the yard? There was no way Henri and his team could defeat them all, even Paul knew that. No, he couldn't be wrong. He was certain: the enemy would come in the morning.

But it already was morning. The time for action was drawing relentlessly nearer.

Paul carefully read through what he had written and signed his name at the bottom of the second page. He folded the letter and slipped it into an envelope, which he sealed and put into an inside pocket of his jacket.

Josette could not sleep; not now.

Outside, the night was still and quiet, but Josette's mind was churning with jumbled thoughts of the day to come and of the people she loved. And of the danger they faced.

She knew their hurriedly cobbled together tactics were far from perfect; they were hardly tactics at all. But thanks mainly to Paul's dogged determination to act while they could, they were going to try to free Julia Bernard.

Josette was afraid – not for herself, but for the others, especially her father. He'd changed; she'd realized that during the evening. He'd suddenly grown older. He was in his late forties, so wasn't old, but the many stresses and the anguish of the last year seemed finally to have taken their toll.

During the meeting, once Henri had virtually confessed that he was bereft of ideas, it had been Paul and Didier, particularly Paul, who had taken the initiative. Henri had been far less decisive than he used to be. If it came to a fight in the morning, that hesitancy could be fatal. They were all at risk, but Henri, perhaps, most of all.

Josette sighed and pulled the blanket up to her chin, not because she was sleepy, but because the soft wool against her face was comforting. She desperately wanted to protect the man who had been her protector for the past seventeen years. It was a strange thought, upsetting. Her father had always considered her his little girl, the baby of the family. And despite her many loud and frequent protestations, sometimes she had secretly quite liked it.

But she wasn't Henri's little girl any more; she had grown up.

The war had made her grow up, and made her father grow old.

Didier had much to consider. They had decided on the tactics and logistics of the raid on the wood yard, but there was still the personnel to worry about.

With the exception of Inigo, they were all novices in the type of guerrilla warfare they were planning: hit and run, get in and get out before the enemy had a chance to respond.

Inigo himself admitted that even for him it had been a long time, but Didier instinctively felt that the little Spanish terrier would still acquit himself well. Inigo would be at the forefront of the action, as would Didier and Paul. And Paul was the one Didier was most worried about.

He'd become more and more reckless in his actions: charging into the barn as he did could have ended in disaster. And though, thankfully, he'd got away with it, he still didn't seem to fully appreciate that it had been a crazy move even though it gained them the vital information they needed. Paul had been lucky, and luck didn't always hold. It turned, usually without warning.

Didier reminded him again that they were up against a team of highly trained professional soldiers. But Paul's judgement was clouded by the desire to beat the enemy while he had the chance. And the next impulsive or impetuous move might prove deadly, for them all.

Didier was going to have to keep a close watch on him, as well as look out for his own safety. They were the best of friends, in many ways closer than brothers. They worked side by side at the factory, spent most of their spare time together, shared a sense of humour and they were both crazy about Josette, although they tended not to mention that fact in their conversations.

But in wartime, situations change quickly and now Paul was leaving, probably forever. A Lysander would swoop in to Puivert in less than twenty-four hours; *Eagle* really was going to happen, as long as Paul made it to the rendezvous point on time.

Didier told himself that he was going to make sure that Paul not only got there on time, but that he also got there in one piece.

Henri sat in an armchair, rhythmically smoothing down the bristles of his bushy moustache with the index finger of his right hand. He was very worried and very anxious.

He was in charge of the operation, and the responsibility was weighing heavily on his shoulders. Josette; Paul and Didier; Inigo; Max and Julia Bernard; his mother, Odile; his wife, Hélène; even Didier's mother had been dragged into this now. No one had complained.

Henri wanted to inspire them all, to fill them with confidence with stirring words and daring deeds. But he didn't feel confident. He was far from confident.

He had never particularly wanted to lead the Resistance group, but when they'd started it the previous year, there was no one else prepared to do the job. That's what the others said, anyway. They voted him leader. He was proud, in his own modest way, and thought he merited his code name.

But these days he was almost always tired, and he'd started to think that he no longer had the energy, the skill or even the imagination to lead. And the cunning of Reynard the fox seemed to have deserted him.

Sitting there in the armchair, he told himself that he must think positively. They would win through, and when this operation was over he would hand the group over to Didier. He would still be there to advise, to discuss and help where he could, but the running of the group needed to be in the hands of a younger man.

And of course there was Josette. Even with Didier in charge, she would still have plenty to say about how the group was run. Despite his worries, Henri realized that he was smiling at the thought of his beloved daughter. Josette would always be his little girl.

Max Bernard watched Inigo pour fuel into the empty glass bottle. There was a row of filled bottles now, all with screw tops securely tightened. In the morning, if and when the home-made incendiary devices were required, the screw tops would be removed and a cloth wick soaked in alcohol would be pushed into the neck of each bottle and made secure by a cork. The wick would be lit, the bottle hurled at the target, and when it smashed on impact it would create an instant fireball as the flame ignited the fuel. It was an effective weapon, and highly dangerous for both the intended victims and the thrower.

"I made many of these in the Civil War," Inigo said quietly, watching the last of the fuel trickle into the bottle. "More than I could count. We all used them; us, Franco's forces. They're very dangerous, I've seen them explode in people's hands."

"Are you sure you want to take the risk, Inigo? This isn't your fight."

Inigo smiled grimly. "It is my fight; it's everyone's fight." He tightened the screw top. "And I'm an expert with these things. You have to be quick, because once the wick is alight the thrower becomes very visible to the enemy, a clear target. So you get as close as you can, you light, you throw and you get out fast."

Max looked at the neat row of bottles. They appeared harmless enough, but each one was a bomb. "You know, the Germans want me because they believe I can make them a bomb. I'm an expert, too."

"Yes?" Inigo said, looking impressed. "A bomb like this?"

Max shook his head. "No, not like that, Inigo. A very different bomb, and one that I'll never make."

Victor Forêt huddled uncomfortably in the lumpy chair, beneath a blanket that he was certain had previously been used to keep a horse warm. It stank.

A single oil lamp was burning weakly on the far side of the room, shedding just enough light to see from one wooden wall to the other. The cheap oil burned smokily and made his eyes smart.

Victor detested the house. Wood everywhere, inside and out. The floors, the walls, the ceilings: nothing but wood. It was as though the place had put down roots and grown to become part of the forest. It was desolate and bleak on the brightest of days, but at night, with the sky as black as tar, it seemed the loneliest place in the world.

Victor felt more lonely than he ever had, even though the house was filled to capacity with captives and captors. Most of them were asleep, Victor supposed, but he couldn't sleep no matter how hard he tried.

He was cold and miserable. They'd given him nothing to eat and drink but a few squares of dark German chocolate and a cup of bitter coffee. He wanted – no, he needed – a drink; a beer, or preferably a glass of his favourite red wine. That might help him sleep, and even if it didn't, it would make him feel a lot better.

Victor clicked his tongue irritably and shifted again in the chair. He'd seen no more of the twins. All he knew was that they were locked in one of the upstairs rooms with the Bernard woman.

This just wasn't turning out the way Victor had expected. It would be different in future; the Germans could get on with the war without his help. After this operation, and his final payment, they could keep their money. It wasn't worth the hassle; money wasn't everything. And as far as his principles were concerned, they could change just as they'd changed before. He'd been a Nazi when it suited; now he'd go back to being a patriotic Frenchman.

But never mind the future, it was tomorrow, or rather today, that was worrying Victor the most. He dreaded returning to the café and trying to explain to Celine why he'd been out all night and what he'd been up to. It wasn't completely unheard of for him to stay out for an entire night if he got into a heavy session with some of his old rugby friends. But there were always serious consequences. And whatever he told Celine when he next saw her, he knew she would never believe a word of it. It would turn into a huge row and probably a fight. Another fight.

Victor sighed heavily as he turned from one side to the other, pulling the blanket so that it moved with him. The smell of horse was even stronger. It really did stink; it made him gag, and he groaned in his misery.

Victor really didn't feel well.

Alain Noury hadn't meant to pull the trigger.

He was was fed up, lying on his bed, listlessly staring down the length of his extended arm, aiming the pistol at a framed photograph fixed to a wooden beam, when suddenly it went off.

Alain's arm jerked upwards as the round pierced his mother through the heart and buried itself deep in the beam.

Alain sat up and listened. He wasn't too bothered about the shattered glass or the frame, which had crashed to the floor, or even about shooting his mother. He had plenty more photographs of his mother, boxes full back at the house in Espezel.

What Alain was worried about was the noise. It wasn't a loud pistol, but it was loud enough for anyone nearby to have heard.

It suited Alain to have two homes: the old family house in Espezel and the rooms here in Lavelanet.

The small, scruffy apartment was sparsely furnished, unlike the house in Espezel, and was above a shop close to the centre of town. At this time of the morning the shop was unoccupied, of course, and Alain had no immediate neighbours on either side. The rooms above the shops to either side were used for storage. No one lived in them.

But there were people living close by.

Alain got up from the bed and switched off the dull electric light.

He was fully dressed, but had taken off his shoes, so he tiptoed lightly to the window, trying to avoid the glass splinters on the floorboards.

Cautiously he lifted the curtain and looked out to the street. It was deserted, and Alain was relieved to see that there were no lights on in any of the surrounding buildings.

He smiled: the people of Lavelanet were heavy sleepers. Or perhaps some of them had heard a noise and thought it was a door slamming, or something falling, or a car backfiring.

Or maybe some of them knew they had heard a gunshot and decided not to interfere, to keep their heads down and mind their own business. That was wisest these days.

Alain's smile faded. He wished he had someone to talk to about the way he was feeling. But there was no one. His parents were dead, but he'd never conversed with them much anyway; they'd been simple country people who'd just got on with their lives. He had no brothers or sisters, and no real friends any more. There had been one, Yves Bessont, but they'd been more like drinking buddies than actual friends. Then they'd had a big row in a bar, and now they didn't even speak if they spotted each other in the street. Gaston and Yvette were never friends, but at least back then he'd been part of something.

Now there was nothing. Even his twin cousins were not close friends. They tolerated him, indulged him, shared a beer now and then, but they didn't really like him. Alain knew that. He wasn't stupid.

Alain turned away from the window, took a couple of cautious steps and sat down on his bed. He'd been deep in thought just before the pistol went off, getting angry with Victor Forêt and then with Henri Mazet and his whole crowd.

"That's it," he said aloud, and felt his anger rising again.

Now he was furious.

Hauptmann Kurt Lau took a deep drag of his cigarette as he stood in the wood yard looking back to the house. Dull light shone from one downstairs window, but the rest of the building was in darkness. As dark as the night, which was ink black.

Low cloud shifted quickly across the sky, blocking out the starlight. Lau gazed up, hoping that the weather forecast for the coming day was right, and that by first light the clouds would have cleared completely.

The sounds of the night forest cut through the still air: the rustle and snuffle of nocturnal predators hunting for their victims, a fir cone striking a branch on its way to the ground, birds stirring and shaking their feathers before settling again.

The forest never slept.

Lau did not want to sleep either. He was glad to have taken his turn on guard duty. He often did; it was good for team morale. And Lau sensed that morale in the team was not at its highest. That was hardly surprising; there had been bad luck and a series of mistakes. That's what came of depending on paid informers and traitors.

But Lau was confident that he would put things right. He had a fine reputation and the military honours and decorations to prove it. No mission of his had ever ended in total failure. Some had not gone completely to plan, of course; that was only to be expected in war. War was unpredictable; there were always difficulties, and sometimes even serious setbacks.

But setbacks had to be met head-on and overcome. Lau remained confident and convinced that in the coming hours everything would fall into place and his mission would succeed. His fine reputation, so hard won, would remain intact.

Across the yard, twenty metres away, the back door of the house opened and Erich Steidle emerged. He noiselessly closed the door and stood staring into the night.

Lau was cloaked in darkness, in the shadows of the trees and the cover of the clouds. He took a silent drag at his cigarette and waited. Steidle walked straight to him. He saluted. "My watch, sir. You need to get some rest."

Lau smiled and took a final drag at his cigarette. The lit end glowed like a tiny beacon.

TWENTY-EIGHT

When the Brandenburgers went into action, they made an impressive sight. Every man had a designated task and each unit functioned like clockwork.

The two teams had synchronized watches; they were hitting the two houses at exactly the same moment; if they had telephones, Lau wouldn't allow anyone in either house the slightest opportunity to make a hurried warning call to the other.

It was soon after first light. The lorry was parked just down the street from Henri Mazet's house when Lau and two of his men, the Brothers Grimm as they called themselves, passed noiselessly through the unlocked gate in the back garden and hurried across the damp grass to the back door.

The doors and windows were firmly shuttered, but Lau had anticipated that. He watched as a small explosive charge was fixed to the back door shutters. As the fuse burned down, the Brandenburgers took cover. Lau was taking a calculated risk. The house was detached, surrounded by a high walled garden, and was a reasonable distance from its nearest neighbours. Lau had decided that even though the explosion might be heard by neighbours, it would be worth it in terms of the confusion it caused among those inside the house.

Speed and shock were the tactics: no one would get the chance to react and fight back.

Lau had his pistol at the ready; the two soldiers were armed with rifles.

The charge went off, loud but not thunderous, and the shutters disintegrated in a hail of splinters and shattered glass.

Lau and the other soldiers charged, kicking in what little remained of the back door and sprinting through the kitchen into the hallway. No one appeared at the top of the stairs. The Brandenburgers went rushing up the wide staircase.

Lau was at the front. He ran to the door furthest from the top of the stairs to ensure that no one got in anyone else's way. He pushed open the door, pistol raised, and at the same moment heard his two men burst into the rooms back along the corridor.

Lau stared. There was no one in the darkened room. The bed was made and looked as though it had not been slept in. Fearing the worst, he stepped back to the corridor as his men emerged from other rooms. Both shook their heads.

There were only two more doors on the first floor, but Lau was already certain that the house was deserted as he went into the bathroom and then a final bedroom. They too, were empty.

"Search the place!" Lau barked to one of his men.

"But there's no one here, sir."

"I know that! You're looking for clues. Something to tell us where they are; what they're doing." There was a hint of desperation in his voice. "Anything!"

Erich Steidle, accompanied by Rudi Werner, had chosen a different method from his boss. He was the leader of his two-man team, and it was up to him to dictate the operational tactics. Speed and stealth were his key words.

He was at the rear of Odile Mazet's house while Werner waited near the front door, ready to stop anyone from fleeing that way.

The house, an old, end-of-terrace stone-built cottage close to the River Touyre, was much smaller than Henri's. It was two-up and two-down, with a little glass-roofed lean-to on the back. And there were no shutters on either the door to the lean-to or the one to the kitchen. So there was no need for explosives.

Using his knife, Steidle forced the simple lock on the lean-to door. The rushing sound of the swiftly flowing river easily covered the slight creak of the door opening.

Steidle moved inside and found the back door equally easy to force. He entered the kitchen and paused, listening. Somewhere a clock was ticking, but there was no other sound. Swiftly but silently, he mounted the stairs; one of them creaked, but he reached the landing too soon for anyone to have time to react.

He pushed open the first door, a bedroom. It was empty.

He went to the second door and tried the handle. The door was locked.

Steidle stood back, raised one leg and smashed the heel of his boot against the woodwork. The door held. With the second kick it went crashing down.

The room was empty; the bed was made and had not been slept in.

The Brandenburger hurried down the stairs and unlocked the front door, where Werner was waiting. Steidle gestured to Victor Forêt's car. "Let's go."

Victor was sitting in the back seat, peering out nervously through the rear window. He was afraid. He'd been bundled into his own car and ordered to sit in the back and stay quiet.

The Germans got into the car, Steidle in the driver's seat. "We're going to Mazet's house; tell me the way as I drive."

The car roared away. A few minutes later it passed the parked lorry and went through the open iron gates at Henri Mazet's house.

"Out!" Steidle bawled at Victor.

"But—"

"Out!"

Victor hauled himself from the car and was manhandled into the house.

Lau was waiting in the hallway. He cursed as Steidle shook his head.

"Where is he?" Lau breathed ominously to Victor.

"You mean Bernard? I don't know! How would I know? I thought he would be here or at Mazet's mother's place. It's what you thought, too."

"Are you playing me for a fool? Is that it? Double dealing?"

"*No!* I'm loyal to you. I told you, I'm a Nazi, I believe in everything you … in everything the Führer believes in."

"Then how has he escaped us again? And where are Mazet and his family? Did you tip them off?"

"No! How could I, I've been with you! Perhaps … perhaps Mazet is at his factory."

Lau was seething. "We can't go there and make ourselves known, we might as well tell the whole town the German army is here! If they don't know already!"

One of Lau's men came hurrying down the staircase. He was carrying a radio transmitter, which was fitted snuggly into a brown leather attaché case. "Found this under the floorboards in one of the bedrooms, sir."

Lau glared at Victor. "You're right about something at last! Henri Mazet is Resistance."

Victor felt his heart thumping in his chest. "Can I go home now, please?"

TWENTY-NINE

Otto Berg heard the shattering of glass and then wood splintering. The fools: they were trying to escape through the single small window in the room, smashing out glass and frame. They were going to jump for it.

Berg had climbed the stairs with bread and three cups of coffee on a tray; the prisoners had had nothing to eat since early the previous evening. Berg was tough like all the Brandenburgers, but he wasn't heartless, and as he'd not been ordered to starve the prisoners to death, he'd decided to give them a drink and a bite to eat. But he wouldn't take unnecessary risks. His pistol was in one hand and the tray was in the other.

The rule in this situation was to order the prisoners to stand away from the door, which he would unlock and open. Once he was certain they were at a safe distance, he would place the tray on the floor. One prisoner was permitted to come and pick up the tray and then move back so that the door could be closed and relocked. Simple: it was the accepted procedure.

But procedure had suddenly changed. Berg heard wood splinter again and guessed that the window was probably out. He had to move fast. There was no time to chase back down the stairs and sprint all the way around to the front of the house; all three might well have disappeared into the forest by then.

He put down the tray, whipped out the key to the room and unlocked the door. Turning the handle, he pushed open the door and saw one of the twins and Julia Bernard where the window and frame had been until a few seconds earlier.

The twin was in the process of helping Julia Bernard climb out through the gap.

"Stop!" Berg yelled, realizing that the other twin must already have jumped. "Stop or I'll drop you both!"

Gilbert Noury instantly raised his hands. "No, please, don't shoot!"

"Get down from the window," Berg screamed at Julia. "Both of you, back away! Now!"

Julia climbed down without speaking. She raised her hands too.

"Quick, over there," Berg shouted, indicating with his pistol where he wanted them to go so that he could get to the gaping hole to catch sight of the second twin before he disappeared into the forest.

Hands raised, Gilbert and Julia slowly edged backwards across the room.

Once he was satisfied that they were far enough away,

Berg stepped further into the room.

He never knew what hit him.

He was halfway across the room, eyes fixed on Gilbert and Julia, when Eddie stepped from behind the open door and cracked him across the back of the head with a chair leg.

Berg didn't scream in pain; he just dropped like liquid, out cold.

"That one's for the dog," Eddie said, tossing the chair leg aside and kneeling to check on the German.

"It wasn't him who killed the dog," Gilbert said.

Eddie looked up at his brother. "You think I care which one it was? They did it."

"Is he dead?" his brother asked, picking up the pistol that had dropped from Berg's hand.

A lump the size of a chicken's egg had already appeared on Berg's head. "No," Eddie said. "He'll live."

"Tie him up and we'll get out of here."

The rope that had been used to tie the twins' hands was on a chair. Eddie snatched it up and began binding the unconscious man's hands and feet.

Berg suddenly groaned and opened his eyes a little. They were glassy and unfocused.

Eddie smiled as he continued with his work. "Think you know everything, you Germans. But you shouldn't have been kind and untied us last night, my friend. A big mistake."

Berg's gaze seemed to fix on Eddie for a few seconds, but then his eyes rolled back in his head and he slipped back into unconsciousness.

"Eddie, we need to move," Gilbert said. "We don't know how long we've got before the others come back."

Julia had been staring out through the hole in the wall where the window had been. "But where will we go?" she asked, looking back at Gilbert.

"We could take the police car if it's still in the barn, and I'd guess it is. The Germans said yesterday it was too risky for them to use it again, but it's a risk for us, too."

"But we'd get away from here."

"Yeah, and if we get halfway down the track and run into the Germans coming the other way we're in big trouble. Our best chance is to strike out through the forest, go deeper and move down towards Bélesta. No one knows the forest like Eddie and me. Eh, Eddie?"

"Know every tree by name," Eddie said with a grin as he got to his feet. "Let's go."

He spotted the coffee cups as they moved on to the landing. He picked one up and took a sip, and immediately spat the black liquid out onto the floorboards. "Those Germans make lousy coffee, too."

THIRTY

Lavelanet market, like most markets in Southern France, started early and was generally finished by midday. Traders would arrive on site while it was still dark, putting up their stalls and setting out their wares, ready for the first shoppers on the prowl for bargains soon after sunrise.

But Lavelanet market was never just about shopping; it was also a major social occasion, where friends met for a chat and a gossip or a friendly argument over coffee or a glass of wine. When the weather was fine, the market was at its busiest and so were the cafés. And the weather forecasters in both England and Germany were right so far with their predictions for the day; the spring sun was already climbing in a cloudless sky.

It was still very early when Victor Forêt and the Brandenburgers arrived, but the market was heaving. Victor had completely lost track of the days, and was almost as surprised as the Germans to see the hundreds of shoppers milling about the long street where the market took place.

"Celine!" Victor gasped. "She'll kill me." Lau was at his side, with two more of the Brandenburgers just behind, edging forward, eyes scanning the crowd. The two remaining members of the team were a little further back.

"If we don't find Bernard, then *I* might very well kill you," Lau murmured.

"But I never leave Celine alone in the café on market day. She can't cope."

"Then find me Bernard!" Lau hissed. "Or someone who will lead me to him."

Back at Henri's house, Lau had decided that as a last-ditch measure they would search the streets close to where Victor had spotted Bernard with Odile and Josette. They might just see him or, perhaps more likely, Odile Mazet or one of her family, who might lead them to their target.

It was a slim chance – Lau knew he was clutching at straws – but with time running out and nothing else to go on, he thought it worth a try. And if by some chance they got a sighting of Max Bernard but had no chance to snatch him, there was still the back-up option of putting a bullet in his brain. Lau would sanction the killing if there was no other choice. He had his orders.

They had piled into the two vehicles only to arrive at the heaving market a few minutes later. Lau instantly changed his plan again, deciding that searching a crowd might be more profitable than driving up and down deserted streets.

He ordered his men to keep their mouths shut and told

the frightened Victor to stay right by his side.

All the Brandenburgers had seen photographs of Max Bernard, but only Victor had seen him for real, and only Victor would be able to recognize Odile Mazet, her granddaughter, Josette, and her son, Henri, if any of them were at the market.

"The boy, Paul, who lives with Mazet," Victor said quietly to Lau as they moved slowly between the stalls, "arrived here last year with some story about learning the textile trade; he has to be involved in the Resistance cell. And there's Didier Brunet: I've always had my suspicions about him. Didier and Josette were in my café only the other day, watching me like hawks."

Lau grabbed Victor by the arm and pulled him to a halt in the space between two stalls. The other Brandenburgers crowded around to prevent anyone from getting too close and overhearing what was being said.

"Why didn't you tell me any of this before?"

"You … you didn't ask. And I didn't think it was important."

"Everything's important, and I need to know! Did they overhear you saying something to someone? Anything? Think, man, is there anything more you can tell me?"

Victor's brow creased. "It was when I was having the argument with Alain Noury, the cousin of the twins. They saw me throw him out, that's all. But the Mazet girl was looking down her nose at me like I'm dirt, like she always does."

Lau thought for a moment. "And the Mazet girl and her family were not at home this morning, and her grandmother was not at her home. They knew we were coming. They knew."

Odile Mazet carefully steered her daughter-in-law, Hélène, and Didier's mother, Virginie, away from the small huddle of men between the two market stalls.

She'd glimpsed the man with Victor Forêt pull him aside and saw the others quickly cluster around them. Odile knew instantly who they were. Walking away, she smiled; if Victor had taken just a few paces more they would have come face to face.

Odile and Hélène had spent the night with Virginie Brunet after Henri took Paul and Didier's advice and decided that none of his family should remain in their homes. Didier escorted the two women to his mother's house, where he swiftly explained matters to Virginie, who accepted the situation instantly and without complaint. Then, before leaving to bed down with everyone else at Inigo's cottage, Didier suggested another security precaution: "Leave the house early, and spend the morning in the market, Mama."

"You know I always go to the market, and early," his mother said. "But why should we stay the whole morning?"

"Because it's easiest to hide in a crowd," Didier replied, kissing his mother goodbye. "The Germans won't think to come here, but just in case they do, go out early and stay out all morning, until the market's over."

The women had taken Didier's advice, and all seemed to be going well until the sharp-eyed Odile spotted Victor and his new friends approaching. She hadn't needed to explain to Hélène and Virginie why she was guiding them in a different direction so quickly.

"I think we'll go and get a coffee, don't you, ladies?" she asked as they reached the boundary of the market area.

"Yes, but we'll give Victor's café a miss, eh?" Hélène said with a smile.

"And we'll take our time," Virginie said. "Perhaps we'll make it two coffees. And a croissant if they have them."

Victor and the Germans had reached the other end of the market. Victor's café was no more than a hundred metres away, and for a moment he considered making a bolt for it. Even the prospect of facing Celine's fury was better than the ordeal he was suffering. But the thought was only fleeting. He knew such a move would be fatal and Victor wanted very much to live.

Several shoppers and market traders had nodded a greeting, some voicing their surprise that Victor was not at his usual station behind the bar. One or two had even stopped to chat, but each time Lau muttered a few words to the plump, sweating café owner before nudging him onward.

As they turned to retrace their steps, Erich Steidle stepped closer to Lau. He spoke very quietly, trying not to reveal his less than perfect French accent to any passers-by. He also dropped the customary "sir" to avoid arousing suspicion. "May I say something?"

"Of course."

"I've been thinking; both houses empty this morning, and no sign of Henri and his people here – is it possible they might try to … get to … our friend's wife?"

Lau's face registered his concern. "Get to her? At the wood yard, you mean?"

Steidle nodded.

"But how would they know we're based there?"

Steidle shrugged. "They seem to know a lot more than we've been giving them credit for. It's just a thought."

Lau consider again. "We'll get back there. Quickly."

He grabbed Victor by the arm and propelled him forward into the crowd.

Alain Noury watched them move away.

He'd been hanging around the market since it opened for business, watching the crowd swell, hoping to get a sighting of Victor. And now he had.

But Victor was with the two strangers he'd met up on the plateau with his cousin, Gilbert. And there were more strangers, too, and one of those might well have been the man he'd seen in the truck with his cousin the previous day.

They were obviously searching for something or someone.

It was all too unsettling; Alain did not like not knowing what was going on. He didn't like it at all. He was becoming angry all over again. Very angry.

He followed Victor and his newfound friends.

At a safe distance.

THIRTY-ONE

Morning came slowly to the forest. The waiting was long and anxious.

Paul and Didier knew their tactics for the coming rescue attempt needed equal amounts of good luck and good timing.

For a start, Paul's calculated guess that the majority of the German force would be out searching for Max needed to be right. And they wouldn't have any clues about that until they got a sighting of the house and yard.

But they'd fixed on their plan, and once the light was good enough for them to pick their way through the gloom of the forest they had to get on with it.

Henri's car and Didier's motorbike were tucked away in a small track that quickly petered out into a dead end. The vehicles could not be seen from the road.

Soon they would split into the three teams of two that had been decided on the previous night: Paul and Didier, Inigo and Josette, Henri and Max. Each team had a designated task.

Paul and Didier's job was to make the rescue once the

diversion had been created. That was down to Inigo, with Josette helping as necessary.

Inigo was to explode two petrol bombs halfway along the track, out of sight from the house and far enough away for any Germans inside to have to come out to investigate.

And in the minutes that any remaining guard or guards were away from the house, Paul and Didier would go in and bring Julia out.

The Noury twins also had to be taken into consideration, but Paul reckoned they would so grateful at being freed that they would immediately join forces with their rescuers. At least, he hoped they would

Inigo had argued briefly for more direct action, saying they should ambush the Germans and attack them with petrol bombs. But Henri, backed up by everyone else in the team, had swiftly vetoed this idea. It was far too dangerous and almost certainly doomed to failure.

The team was armed with nothing more than Didier's shotgun and Inigo's petrol bombs. They'd considered taking knives or clubs of some sort, but eventually even Inigo agreed that if it came to hand-to-hand combat with the German soldiers they would have no chance at all, so that idea was abandoned.

Henri and Max were to remain hidden close to the entrance to the track, near the road. Henri was carrying an old metal whistle, which he had kept since serving with the French army during the First World War.

The whistle had a grim history, having been used in the battlefield trenches to warn of gas attacks. It would be employed as a warning device on this operation too. Henri would sound a long blast in the event of anyone, German or otherwise, driving on to the track to approach the yard. The sound would carry all the way to the house.

Max had tried to insist that he be one of those going in for the rescue attempt, but once again, Henri, backed by Didier and Paul, had said no.

"You're a scientist, Max," he told him, "not a fighter. And anyway, you're too emotionally involved; you might do something rash if you sense your wife is in danger. Tomorrow is a time for cool heads for us all."

Didier had said nothing at the time, but he glanced towards Paul with a meaningful look and Paul had nodded his understanding; this included him.

So the plan was fixed. It needed synchronized timing; Paul and Didier had to be in position and ready for the rescue when Inigo exploded the first petrol bomb. They knew that from the roadside entrance of the track to the back of the house was just over a kilometre, and Josette surprised everyone by confidently announcing during the meeting that it took exactly twelve minutes to walk a kilometre.

"How do you know that?" Didier asked her.

"I just do."

"But how can you be certain?"

"Because I've timed myself doing it several times."

Didier looked puzzled. "Why would you do that?"

"Because I wanted to, that's why," Josette said indignantly. "And it's fortunate for us that I have, isn't it, now that we need to know how long it takes."

Didier didn't argue any more and they decided, because of the rough forest terrain, to allow Paul and Didier twenty minutes to reach their rescue attempt position. If the lorry and Victor Forêt's car were on site, they would know that the full German force was still around, in which case the mission would be aborted. They had reluctantly agreed that trying to fight it out against all the Germans would be nothing short of suicidal.

Aborting the mission was the worst-case scenario, but it had to be considered. If it became reality, Paul and Didier would have a further ten minutes to return to Inigo and Josette at their position halfway along the track. Then they would think again.

Thirty minutes in all. That's how long Inigo would wait before hurling the first petrol bomb to create the diversion. If Paul and Didier were not back with him when those thirty minutes were up, then the operation was on.

It was a thin plan, but it was the only one they had.

They had arrived early, soon after first light, but after the previous day's experience, Paul and Didier knew that blundering around in the semidarkness would be a serious mistake. They had to wait until the daylight was strong enough.

And finally it was.

THIRTY-TWO

The sun was making early forays through the forest canopy by the time Paul and Didier neared the house. They'd left Inigo and Josette in position half a kilometre back down the track. Paul glanced at his watch; thirteen minutes. Plenty of time to reach the back of the yard and check for vehicles.

It was damp underfoot with the morning dew still heavy on the ground when the house came into sharper focus.

Didier was carrying his shotgun. He touched Paul lightly on the arm to bring him to a halt and gestured towards the house. "Look."

Paul followed Didier's eyeline to the first floor of the wooden building and immediately saw the gaping hole in the front wall where a framed window had been.

"It wasn't like that yesterday," Didier said quietly. "Maybe they've already tried to escape."

"Maybe they already *have* escaped," Paul answered.

They hurried on, giving the house a wide berth, and then the yard came into view. There was no sign of any vehicles.

"You're not going to go tearing across the yard again, are you?" Didier asked.

Paul shook his head. "They're not here. They couldn't fit the lorry and Victor's car in the barn, it's too heavily stacked with wood. They've gone searching for Max, just as we thought."

"Just as you thought."

Paul checked his watch again: eighteen and a half minutes. Josette's timings had been good.

Suddenly the shrill blast of a whistle cut through the stillness of the morning like wire through cheese, sending startled birds fluttering from the trees.

"They're coming!" Didier groaned. "We have to abort."

"Not yet," Paul said quickly. "Wait a few minutes; we have to be sure it is the Germans. They won't see us hidden here. If it's them we'll make our escape."

"It won't be anyone else."

"Let's be certain."

They waited as the agonizingly slow seconds turned into a minute and then recognized the heavy growl of a diesel engine.

"The lorry," Didier whispered.

Before Paul had a chance to reply, there was the dull thud of an explosion followed by the whoosh of flames, which leapt into the trees and set the fir needles crackling and flaring.

Paul gasped. "It's Inigo, he's thrown a bomb; he's gone for them!"

The diesel engine roared, and as Paul and Didier stood transfixed, a shot rang out. Then a second explosion rocked the forest.

Birds shrieked and the diesel engine screamed as though the driver was frantically reversing to escape the bomber.

"We've got to help them," Didier said, turning to rush back through the forest.

Paul grabbed his arm. "Wait!" He gestured towards the house; there had been no sign of movement. "Our job is to go in there, check it out, do what we came to do. Julia may be tied up in there, or dead. We have to find out."

"But Josette…"

"Josette would want us to finish the job. That's definite. We have to do it, Didier!"

Without waiting for an answer, Paul ran towards the house as the bark of gunfire echoed through the trees.

Didier hesitated for a moment, then sprinted after Paul, following him in through the open back door.

The kitchen was deserted, but showed clear signs of mass habitation: stacks of dirty plates, unwashed cups and cooking pans; ashtrays filled to overflowing; piles of discarded clothes; and the rank smell of stale food, lamp oil and human sweat.

"Upstairs," Paul said, running for the staircase.

They hurtled up the stairs and immediately saw the wide-open door and the German lying on the floor, arms and legs tied.

He was conscious now, and his eyes widened as they approached. "Untie me," he shouted, "quickly!"

Paul and Didier ignored him as they took in the devastation of the room.

"They've escaped," Paul said. "They got away."

Didier nodded. "Now we can help Josette. Come on!"

They leapt over the prone body of Berg and went hurtling down the stairs.

"Wait!" the German yelled. "Untie me! Please untie me! We'll reward you! Wait!"

THIRTY-THREE
The Battle of Bélesta Forest

It happened so quickly. Josette and Inigo heard the sudden blast of the whistle and exchanged anxious looks. Then the lorry was approaching quickly, with the car close behind.

Josette peered through the trees, trying to get a glimpse of the occupants of the vehicles, when she glanced back and saw Inigo lighting the wick of one of the petrol bombs.

"No, Inigo!" she gasped. "No!"

But it was already too late. Once lit, the bomb had to be thrown.

Inigo's aim was not perfect. The first missile didn't reach the track. It struck a tree, and as the glass shattered and the fuel ignited, there was a blinding flash of light and fir needles fizzed and crackled in a sheet of flame.

Josette saw the car reverse.

Grey ash hung in the air and the stench of petrol and burning wood leaked through the forest. German soldiers were spilling from the lorry; one loosed off a speculative rifle shot as Inigo crouched down and lit a second wick. He hurled the bomb, harder and straighter this time, and it hit the forest floor, exploding close to the lorry. The Germans went to the ground; there were screams of agony.

The driver was still at the wheel, attempting to reverse the heavy vehicle. The engine roared and nearly stalled as the cumbersome lorry rolled backwards off the track and towards the trees, its giant wheels throwing up mud and leaf litter.

Another rifle shot cracked and whistled through the trees, thudding into wood somewhere behind Josette and Inigo. It was way off target; the Germans still hadn't spotted their attackers.

"Inigo, let's go!" Josette hissed. "We have to run for it! Please, Inigo!"

"Not while I've still got this," Inigo growled, snatching his final petrol bomb from the ground.

A contented smile spread over his face as he lit the wick and stood up to throw. "Death to all fascists!"

They were two men down. The Brothers Grimm had been first out of the lorry and had run straight into the blast from the second petrol bomb. Wilhelm, the first out, had suffered significant burns to his face and hands, and Lau knew he had to get him to the house and the emergency medical supplies. Both men needed urgent pain relief; they were lying on the ground writhing in agony.

Lau had been in the car, with Rudi Werner driving and Victor Forêt in the back. Werner acted quickly after the first explosion, reversing the vehicle to what appeared to be a safer position further down the track.

Lau bawled to Victor to stay in the car and stay down. Victor didn't need to be told twice: he sank down in the seat as Lau and Werner ran from the vehicle.

Lau fired a speculative shot into the forest as he kneeled to check on his men, and Werner followed with two further rounds. They were not aiming at anyone, just trying to keep their attacker down, wherever he might be.

Erich Steidle, unused to driving a lorry, had managed to reverse the vehicle off the track through deep muddy ruts, only to come to a sudden and shuddering halt against the massive trunk of a giant fir tree.

The engine stalled and the force of the impact jolted through Steidle's body, sending him jerking forward so that his head cracked against the steering wheel. But Steidle was tough. He didn't bother trying to restart the lorry; his comrades needed him. He leapt from the cab, crouched down and ran across the track.

Werner was in the prone firing position, his eyes raking the forest as he moved the rifle slowly and deliberately through his sight lines. He stopped moving. "I see him," he breathed. "He's mine."

The rifle cracked and there was a distant yell and a scream, and then a third petrol bomb exploded.

Paul and Didier were working their way through the trees, staying alert and aware of the sounds of battle. The last thing they needed was to run straight into five or more heavily armed German soldiers. It would be a massacre.

They moved a stretch at a time, dodging from one place of safety to another, constantly seeking out what cover they could. Didier, carrying the shotgun, led the way, making his ground, checking all around and then gesturing for Paul to join him. It wasn't the fastest way of reaching the action, but Didier, ever cautious, knew it was the safest.

Suddenly they heard running footsteps approaching – no voices, just runners moving much faster than they had managed.

They dived for cover behind the trunk of a fallen tree.

"They're coming straight for us," Didier whispered. He glanced down at the double-barrel shotgun. "If there's more than two of them we're done for."

The runners came closer and closer until they were little more than ten metres away, their footsteps thudding down hard enough for Paul and Didier to feel the vibration through the earth.

Paul nodded to his friend. "Now!"

Didier stood up, bringing the shotgun into the firing position against his shoulder and staring down the barrels.

"Don't shoot!" a voice hissed as two men, both carrying shotguns, slid to a halt on the damp forest floor.

It was the Noury twins.

"Don't shoot!" one of them said again. "We're with you! We're with you!"

* * *

Josette could see about eight centimetres of glass sticking up from her leg. The curved shard narrowed like a slim dagger. It was hard to know how much glass had sliced through her thin trousers and pierced the flesh. But it hurt badly and blood was pumping out steadily.

She had to crawl away and try to find a hiding place; at least one of the Germans was coming for her. She'd heard shouts and then movement.

Now there was silence and all she could hear was her own irregular breathing. But she knew the silence would be brief; they were coming.

She wanted to scream for help, but it was not an option. She had to fight the panic building in her chest. She thought of Paul and Didier and her father. Where were they?

Inigo was dead. The bullet had struck him close to the heart and sent him spinning backwards as the petrol bomb slipped from his grasp. Josette had dived to the ground just in time to avoid being enveloped in the flames. But as the bomb ignited, she had felt the glass slice into her right thigh.

She had to get away, but she couldn't stand. She could hardly even crawl, as the shard was buried deep in the front of her leg. She had to get it out.

She gripped the blood-soaked sliver of glass between her thumb and index finger. Just touching it sent a wave of pain shooting through her leg, and as she tried to pull the glass from her flesh her fingers slid on the blood and she lost her hold.

"Come on, Josette," she breathed. "Do it!"

She clenched the glass again, tighter this time, ignoring the agonizing jolt as she took hold. Closing her eyes, she pulled. The glass came out. It dripped blood and sliced more muscle and flesh on the way, but it came out. Josette opened her eyes to see a fresh spurt of crimson pumping from the wound. She was breathing heavily – and too loudly, she realized.

She dropped the bloodied shard and turned onto her front to crawl further into the forest. Even the slightest movement was painful, and she knew she was leaving a telltale trail of blood as she crawled, but she had to try to get away.

As she edged forward, she saw Inigo less than a metre away, his wide eyes staring at her, his face locked in a contented smile of death.

Josette turned quickly away; she couldn't bear to look. She dragged herself onward, painfully slowly, fearing that at any moment a German would be standing over her with a rifle pointed at her head.

And then another explosion ripped through the air.

The sounds of battle had drawn Henri and Max away from their hiding place at the entrance to the track.

At the first explosion, Henri stared in horror. "My children!"

"Your children?" Max said, confused. "But surely it's only Josette?"

Henri was already running. "They're all my children to me."

He rushed through the trees, unconcerned now for his own safety, with Max hurrying to keep up.

There were shots and a second explosion as they approached Victor Forêt's stationary black Peugeot. From the cover of the trees, Henri glimpsed the rigid figure of Victor in the back seat, but he paid the traitor no heed and ran quickly on. His only thoughts now were for Josette, Paul and Didier. And Henri was terrifyingly aware that his daughter was in the greatest danger.

A rifle shot cracked out, instantly followed by a third explosion then yelling and a scream.

"Josette!" Henri breathed, his face ashen.

The forest was momentarily silent and then there were more yells and shouted orders in German.

Henri reached into the canvas bag he wore over his shoulders and pulled out one of the spare petrol bombs that Inigo had made.

"What are you doing?" Max asked.

"The only thing I can think of doing. Confuse them: draw them away from my daughter and towards us."

Max nodded and watched Henri light the wick.

The sight of the burning fuse seemed to make Henri freeze. He looked at Max and the two men's eyes met.

"Light, throw and get out, that's what Inigo said," Max hissed urgently. "Throw it, Henri, now!"

Spurred into action, Henri drew back his arm and hurled the bomb with all his strength. They dived to the ground and in the next instant heard the explosion and felt the wave of heat as the petrol ignited in a ball of flame.

"Now we get out," Henri said, lifting his head. "And we pray that they follow."

The petrol bomb exploded on the far side of the lorry, shattering a side window in the driver's cab and ripping jagged holes in the canvas covering the back.

As the fuel ignited and the fire blazed, Lau and Steidle instinctively hit the ground, shielding their wounded comrades with their own bodies.

"What the hell is going on?" the officer yelled. "We're surrounded."

"Should I go and look?"

"No! We have to get these men back to the house. They need treatment. And where the hell is Werner?"

Werner was in the forest, hunting down the first bomber, knowing that he'd shot him but not knowing if his shot had been a kill. He was treading slowly and cautiously, eyes peeled, his index finger resting on the rifle's trigger.

He heard the explosion and knew it must have been near the lorry, but he didn't look back. The others would have to deal with that, Werner was focused on taking out the threat in front of him.

Lau and Steidle moved slowly towards the lorry with one

of the wounded men between them. With a great deal of encouragement, he'd managed to stagger to his feet.

Steidle assisted the trembling man to the back of the vehicle while Lau covered them with his raised pistol. The wounded soldier was helped inside and he groaned in pain as his burned limbs made contact with the wooden floor.

"Hold on, Jacob," Lau told him. "We'll get you out of here." He turned to Steidle. "We'll both have to lift Wilhelm – he's unconscious."

"Probably best that he is, sir."

"We need Werner to cover us. Where is Werner!"

Werner hauled Josette to her feet, ignoring her agonized yell as blood pumped from the wound in her thigh.

The Brandenburger turned the terrified girl around, wrapped one arm around her neck and pulled her close so that his face was against hers. "How many of you?" he hissed into her ear.

Josette could smell the soldier's sour breath. She said nothing and Werner tightened his grip, squeezing until Josette began to struggle for breath. "How many?"

"Find out," Josette managed to gasp.

The Brandenburger glanced back at the body sprawled a few metres away and smiled briefly. His shot had been excellent: a kill. The bomber was dead, but he knew there were more involved in the ambush than the dead bomber and this girl. The last explosion on the far side of the lorry confirmed that.

Werner had the rifle in his free hand. He raised the barrel and rested it against Josette's cheek. "I'll ask you one final time, how many?"

Josette closed her eyes. She wouldn't say another word. She felt faint, dizzy from the loss of blood. She was going to die, she knew it, but she would rather die than betray the others. Her thoughts flicked quickly from her father to her mother and then to Didier and Paul.

She squeezed her eyes tightly shut and thought of Paul.

Paul.

And then she heard his voice.

"Drop the rifle! Drop it!"

Josette opened her eyes in the same moment that Werner wheeled around to see three raised shotguns pointing at his head.

Didier and the Noury twins were all staring down the barrels.

Paul stood between them. "I said, drop it!"

Werner was startled but calm. He was a soldier, a crack soldier and he'd spotted instantly that the weapons aimed at him were all shotguns.

He pulled Josette even tighter to his body, using her as a shield; perfectly secure in the knowledge that there was no way even the best marksman in the world could hit just him with a shotgun. The spread of shot from the cartridge would take out Josette as well. For certain.

Werner glared at the twins. "You two, and a couple of kids. You did all this?"

Eddie returned the glare. "We've only just joined the party."

"But we're glad to be here now," Gilbert continued.

"Won't do you any good," Werner said. "And you won't shoot: kill me and you'll kill this one too." He suddenly squeezed Josette's neck even tighter, causing her to cough and splutter.

"Let her go!" Paul yelled.

For a moment, Didier feared that Paul was going to try to charge the German. "Paul!" he hissed. "Don't!"

Werner laughed. "Your little girlfriend, is she? Well, she's coming with me. We're leaving, so don't even think of trying anything, because if you do, she'll get a bullet in the brain." He laughed again and smiled at Eddie. "Just like your dog, eh?"

He began to move, edging backwards, dragging the helpless Josette with him.

Paul and Didier and the twins could do nothing but watch.

Alain Noury was totally confused.

He'd heard the explosions and the gunfire and instantly dived for cover. Even armed with a pistol of his own, Alain was no hero. He kept his head down as the battle raged.

In Lavelanet he'd followed Victor and the strangers to Victor's Peugeot and the twins' lorry, which was parked behind it. There was no sign of the twins, but when Alain saw the men climb into the vehicles he sprinted to his own van with a good idea of where they would be going.

And he was right. He was on their tail, keeping a very safe distance, before they reached the outskirts of Lavelanet. They were heading for Bélesta, which had to mean they'd continue to the forest and the wood yard. Alain had no need to follow closely.

When he reached the turning, instinct told him not to drive down the track.

He pulled the van off the main road, and as he climbed from the vehicle he heard the dull thud of an explosion and then a shot. He hurtled for cover, like a frightened rabbit.

Since then, hidden in a thicket, he had been vainly trying to work out what was happening. Who were the strangers and who were they fighting? Could it be the twins? And why was Victor Forêt involved?

The fighting had been brief but heavy. Now it had stopped. Completely. There had been no further gunshots or explosions for a full three minutes.

Alain peered nervously from his hiding place.

He waited and watched for movement before finally plucking up the courage to get to his feet and creep on through the trees, staying away from the track.

Soon he glimpsed Victor Forêt's car standing at the edge

of the track. There was no one near it, but as Alain got closer he saw the outline of a figure inside. It was Victor, sitting upright and absolutely still.

Alain grinned. "I see he made sure he kept clear of the fighting," he whispered, conveniently forgetting his own dive for shelter at the first sign of trouble.

He drew his pistol from a pocket and crept closer to the vehicle, staying low, moving silently until he was no more than two metres from the vehicle.

Victor had not spotted him. He was sitting perfectly still, staring forward through the windscreen, obviously afraid that the battle might still come to him.

Alain's smile was even broader this time. He would force Victor to tell him exactly what was going on, but first he was going to enjoy giving him the shock of his life.

Pistol raised, Alain leapt forward, grabbed the handle and yanked open the door, ready to thrust the weapon into Victor's fat, smug face.

"Now, you…!"

Alain stopped mid-sentence and stared.

Victor had not moved. Victor would never move again, at least not by choice. Victor was very obviously dead. His mouth hung open, his staring eyes bulged and one hand rested on his belly just below his heart. It appeared that Victor had suffered a massive heart attack.

"You bastard!" Alain hissed, robbed for good of the pleasure of making Victor squirm in terror. "You bastard!"

His finger tightened on the trigger. It was pointed at Victor's head and Alain desperately wanted to fire.

"Alain!"

Alain almost dropped the Spanish Colt and collapsed as he heard his name whispered.

He spun around and saw Henri Mazet and another man staring at him from the cover of the trees.

Alain's mind was in turmoil. Henri Mazet! Him too? Here? What the hell was going on?

"What are you doing here?" Henri hissed.

"I… I…"

"Did you come to help? You heard the gunfire?"

"I… Victor's dead. A heart attack, I think."

"Come and take cover, the Germans are bound to come back."

"Germans? What…?"

Suddenly, the engine of the lorry rumbled into life further up the track.

"Those Germans," Henri said. "Get in here quickly; they'll come for the car too."

Fear more than anything spurred Alain into rushing into the trees to join the man he considered his other bitter enemy, even though Henri knew nothing of that. Alain was only just quick enough.

As the three men watched, Rudi Werner came sprinting down the track. He spotted the open door of the Peugeot and stopped running. Raising his rifle, he approached the vehicle slowly and peered in through the door.

"Oh, wonderful," he said. "Just what we need."

Werner slammed the door shut, leapt into the driver's seat and started the car. As it bumped off down the rutted track, the three men hidden in the trees saw the lifeless body of Victor Forêt topple over to one side.

THIRTY-FOUR

The battle was over, but the war was far from won.

Henri's battered and weary little army had gathered in a clearing and while one of the twins kept watch, Paul and Didier took stock.

Both sides had suffered casualties and Inigo, fearless but foolhardy, was dead. There were new allies in the twins and, very surprisingly and difficult for Paul and Didier to believe, their cousin, Alain Noury.

Max and Julia Bernard were joyfully reunited. Eddie Noury had quickly fetched Julia from her hiding place once the fighting was over and now the couple were sitting on the ground, holding hands and talking softly, the relief on both their faces plain to see.

But Josette, wounded and afraid, had been taken prisoner.

Henri turned a deathly white when Paul and Didier described how she had been dragged off by the German soldier, bundled into the lorry and driven away to the house. Since then Henri had hardly said a word. He was sitting slumped, head in hands, on a tree stump.

Paul and Didier were trying not to show how frantic with fear they both felt; Paul was wracked with guilt at not getting to Josette sooner. "If I hadn't insisted we go into the house, we'd have reached her before the German," he said to Didier so that Henri did not overhear. "I should have guessed that Julia was safe when we saw the window was out."

"How could you have guessed? No, you were right, we had to go in. And anyway, the German would have picked us all off if we'd come hurtling through the forest armed with nothing more than a few shotguns."

Paul sighed, unconvinced. "We have to get Josette out, somehow. The wound looked bad."

Didier nodded. "I'm glad Henri didn't see it. He looks shattered."

"But we need his orders. We can't sit here doing nothing." Paul turned to Henri and called his name.

Lost in his own anguished thoughts, Henri did not reply.

"Henri?" Paul said again, louder this time.

Henri seemed to barely register their presence as he stared up at them, looking stunned.

"What do we do now, Henri?"

"Rescue my daughter," Henri said in little more than a frightened whisper. "Do whatever you have to, but please rescue my daughter."

Paul and Didier exchanged a look; it appeared that tactical decisions would be down to them.

Eddie was standing guard. His brother and their cousin, Alain, who was explaining how he had come to turn up during the fighting, had joined him. And from what Paul and Didier could overhear, it seemed as though Alain had latched on to Henri's incorrect assumption that he had heard the sounds of battle and bravely rushed in to help his cousins.

"I'd have got to you faster if I'd have known for sure," they heard him boast. "But when I found Victor dead in the back of the car I didn't know what to do. Then Henri Mazet turned up, and then one of the Germans." He lowered his voice to make sure Henri didn't hear. "I'd have taken him out with my pistol, but Henri wouldn't let me."

"He's got a lot more to say than the last time we saw him," Didier said to Paul.

"Do you believe all that?" Paul asked.

"Not really; I never did trust Alain."

They walked over to the twins and their cousin.

"What can you tell us?" Paul asked the twins.

"Everything we know," Eddie said. "We want to make up for what we've done until now."

"Then start at the beginning," Didier said.

Taking turns, the Noury brothers explained how they had come to be involved in the plot to seize Max Bernard and spirit him away to northern France.

They left out nothing: the Germans' arrival on the plateau by parachute, the capture of Julia, the killing of their dog, their imprisonment and eventual escape.

"We did it for the money," Eddie told them, his face flushed with shame, "and we know it was a stupid mistake. We're sorry, truly sorry. I know that's no excuse, but it's the truth. We never intended to be traitors."

"We didn't think it through," Gilbert added. "We're not good at thinking at the best of times, but Victor convinced us it was an easy way to make big money."

"But we're not blaming Victor," Eddie said quickly. "It was our decision, no one forced us into it." He gestured towards Julia. "It was only when she was dragged into the house that we started to realize how stupid we'd been."

"We're not collaborators," Gilbert said, "we're just stupid. Sometimes I think we don't have the brains we were born with."

Paul couldn't stop himself from smiling at the twins' honesty.

"And now Victor's dead; your friend Inigo too," Eddie said. "I took off his jacket and covered his face when I went to fetch Julia. We'll make sure he's buried properly when this is over."

Paul nodded his thanks; it wasn't easy to think of the larger-than-life figure of Inigo laying dead and cold on the forest floor.

"Do you know what the Germans are planning now?" Didier asked Gilbert.

"They spoke about getting out tonight. A plane is picking them up from the plateau."

"Landing on the plateau! Up there!"

"We're meant to be setting the landing torches." He frowned. "We're meant to get our final payment when they leave."

"I'd rather burn their money now," Eddie growled. "The weather's set to turn, so they won't put it off; they'll go tonight if they can."

"Exactly as you predicted," Didier said to Paul.

Paul shrugged his shoulders, thinking quickly. "We have to use it to our advantage now. And we've got three things in our favour."

"And they are?"

"One and two; they don't know how many we are or how well armed we are."

"They saw three shotguns and they heard the petrol bombs."

"But they don't know that's all we have. Our best weapon is bluff; make them believe we're a bigger and better armed force than we actually are."

"But what if Henri's daughter tells them the truth?" Eddie asked.

"Josette will tell them nothing," Paul said sharply.

"Nothing," Didier echoed.

Gilbert looked at Paul. "You said three things in our favour – what's the third?"

"Actually, it's four things. Three and four are you and your brother."

"Us?"

"The Germans need you to get away, and I've got an idea. So we'll make them an offer; in exchange for Josette they get safe passage from the forest and you two going with them to the plateau to light the landing strip. Exactly as they wanted."

Gilbert's face clouded. "But we told you, we won't help them again."

"You'll be helping us and getting rid of them," Paul argued. "And there's no point in more fighting if we can avoid it. We won't beat them that way."

Gilbert shrugged his broad shoulders. "Maybe you're right, maybe it's worth a try."

Eddie gestured towards Max and Julia. "But what about them? He's what this is all about. If the Germans know he's around, they might still try to grab him."

Gilbert nodded in admiration. "Sometimes, little brother, you're not as stupid as you look."

"And he's right," Didier said. "The Germans put a lot of money and effort into this operation. They want Max badly. We should get the two of them away from here now."

"But where to? Where do they go?" Paul said.

"We'll take them to Antoine and Rosalie Granel at Bélesta. They'll be safe there until this is all over."

Paul nodded. "It's a good idea, but we've only got Henri's car; we'll need that ourselves."

Alain Noury had said nothing during the exchange, but

he'd been listening intently to every word.

"I can take them," he said, smiling. "My van's at the end of the track. I'll take them to Bélesta if you want."

THIRTY-FIVE

Rudi Werner had always secretly wanted to be a sniper. The Brandenburgers were a special outfit and he felt privileged to be part of the regiment, but to be a sniper: that was extra special. That was Iron Cross territory.

A sniper was a man apart, working alone, taking orders from no one, ice-cool in all circumstances, living or dying by his own split-second decisions.

Snipers were a special breed. Snipers, Rudi Werner thought, were men like him.

Werner had twice before applied to join the elite group of individuals drawn from all parts of the army. Both times he had been one hundred per cent successful on the firing range, but both times he'd been rejected after his interview. He was disappointed, but not downhearted. He knew it was only a matter of time before all his qualities were fully recognized.

Werner was perched on the first floor of the farmhouse, hidden behind an upturned chair in the space where the bedroom window had been until earlier that day. He felt at ease, like a sniper.

In the prone position, looking down the barrel of his rifle, he had a perfect view of the track and entire forest area to the front of the house. His rifle was at the ready, a pistol was on one side for back-up, and in an emergency there were stick grenades on the other side. But they wouldn't be necessary; there would be no emergency.

Let them come, however many there were; Werner was ready.

He'd pick off the twins like he'd picked off their dog. And that pushy kid who'd tried to give him orders in the forest, he'd put one right between his eyes if he showed his face.

Josette was puzzled by the man leading the German soldiers. She'd imagined that all Germans were like the brute who'd grabbed her and thrown her into the back of the lorry, but this man was being surprisingly kind and gentle. He had even smiled when she at first refused to tell him her name.

"Military prisoners of war are permitted to give their name and number when captured," he told her in perfect French.

Josette hesitated for a moment longer before speaking. "It's Josette."

Lau smiled again. "Well, Josette, you have a deep cut in your leg and you've lost a lot of blood. I'm not a doctor, but I do have some training as a medic, so if you'll allow me, I'll clean it and patch you up as best I can."

"Thank you," Josette said. She was sitting back in an old armchair, which was fortunate, because she felt as though she might pass out at any moment.

She watched as the soldier took a knife and began to cut at the material of her ripped trousers.

"I'm afraid these are ruined anyway," he said.

Josette turned her head away. The large kitchen looked more like the emergency ward of a hospital. Lau had attended to his own men first. The most badly burned was unconscious, and even Josette could tell that his injuries were severe. He was shivering as he slept.

The other burned man was in better shape. He was lying on a makeshift bed, smoking and exchanging a few words in German with a third man, whose head had been bandaged. He was smoking too. A fourth soldier was standing by the open door with a rifle in his hands, watching the yard.

Josette winced as the officer dabbed carefully at her wound with gauze soaked in antiseptic fluid.

"I'm sorry," he said quietly, not looking up, but continuing to clean the wound. "The stitches will hurt even more, and I'm afraid they will leave a scar."

"I don't care about that and I don't care about it hurting."

"You're very brave."

Josette's famously short temper flared. "Are you laughing at me?"

Lau glanced up at her. "Certainly not."

"Good. And I'm not crying. My eyes are watering because of the smoke from those disgusting cigarettes."

"Of course, I understand. They are rather strong, but in the circumstances I think I must allow my men to smoke. They too are very brave."

The stitches were excrutiating, but Josette gritted her teeth until the wound was tightly closed.

Lau nodded in satisfaction. "Not a perfect job, but not too bad."

"Thank you."

This time Josette watched as Lau cleaned around the wound again before starting to wrap a bandage around her leg.

"The man who was shot," he said as he worked, "was he a relation of yours?"

"A friend."

"And are there many more friends waiting for us out there?"

Even though she felt disorientated, Josette was still aware enough to be definite with her reply. "I can't tell you that."

Lau smiled. "I understand."

"My friend, the one who was shot," Josette said after a few moments, "he hated Nazis. I … I do, too, but … I'm grateful to you for stitching up my leg."

Lau finished the bandaging and secured the dressing with a pin. He looked up at Josette. "Perhaps we have more in common than you know."

"I don't understand."

The officer smiled again. "Never mind. I hope your leg heals well. It will be sore for a while. And you must drink plenty of fluids and be careful that your temperature does not rise. You probably need a blood transfusion, but as I said, I'm no doctor. I'll fetch you some water."

He got up and went to the doorway, where Erich Steidle stood guard.

Lau spoke in German. "It seems we've lost this time, Erich."

Steidle kept his eyes on the forest. "What now, sir?"

"We get out tonight if we can."

"Did she tell you anything?"

"The girl?"

Steidle nodded.

"No. And I'm not going to interrogate her; she's just a kid."

Steidle had a different opinion. "She helped take out two of our comrades. Good men."

Lau gazed out to the treeline, thinking. "We'll wait until dark and take her with us to the landing site. They won't fire on us if they know she's in the lorry, and we'll make certain they do."

"I could go out now, scout around; see if I can find out exactly how many we're up against."

Lau shook his head. "I need you here, Erich."

"And the landing torches, sir?"

"They're in the barn somewhere. It's too risky to go for them now; our friends out there must be watching the back as well as the front. We'll find the torches after dark."

He saw the look of doubt cross his second-in-command's face.

"We'll find a way, Erich," he said, "we always do."

"And what about Wilhelm, sir? Will he make it?"

Lau looked over at the unconscious soldier. "I don't know. I think his body has gone into shock; that's as potentially fatal as the actual burns. And moving him will only make it worse."

THIRTY-SIX

Henri suddenly leapt up from the tree stump and announced that he was ready to take command again.

"I'm sorry," he told Paul and Didier, "I was thrown off balance when you told me about Josette, completely off balance. But I'm all right now, and ready to go on. Tell me what plans you've been making."

Paul glanced at Didier and raised his eyebrows. Henri didn't look all right, and he certainly didn't sound all right. His eyes were wild, darting from one person to another, and both hands were bunched into tight fists. He looked and sounded like a bag of nerves ready to burst.

"We do have a plan," Didier said gently as they moved a little away from the others so that they could speak privately, "and we're confident we can make it work ..." He hesitated for a moment. "... without you, Henri. We think you should rest for a bit longer, don't we, Paul?"

"Nonsense," Henri said, before Paul had the chance to speak. "I've been leaving far too much to you two over the past couple of days. It's my responsibility; Josette is my responsibility. I'm leading this operation."

"But…"

"Tell me the plan," Henri ordered with uncharacteristic sharpness. "Quickly. We mustn't waste any more time."

Reluctantly, but realizing there was no other choice, Paul outlined their idea.

But it seemed as though Henri was hardly listening to Paul's words. He fidgeted anxiously throughout the explanation, impatient to speak again. "Yes … yes," he said, "it could work. I'll negotiate; they can't possibly want to take my daughter with them. She'll only be in their way."

"But the twins are useful to them," Didier said. "They can actually help them get off the plateau tonight."

"And we must let them know for certain that we don't intend to jeopardize their departure," Henri said, clearly agitated. "It's only Josette we're interested in now; we must get her to safety."

Didier glanced quickly at Paul. "Yes, Henri, we know that. We also thought it would be best to get Max and Julia away from the forest. Then we … you … can tell the Germans that there's no longer any possibility of finding him."

"Yes, yes, we'll do that, too," Henri agreed. "Keep everything simple, that's best."

Paul gestured over towards Alain Noury. "He's offered to drive them to Bélesta in his van, to the Granels, but we don't think it's a good idea."

"Why not?"

"We don't think he can be trusted."

"That's unfair, Paul," Henri said shortly. "I've had my differences with Alain in the past, but on this occasion I'm full of admiration. He heard the shooting and when he realized his cousins were in danger, he hurried to help. That takes courage."

"I've never thought of Alain Noury as someone with courage," Didier said.

"Perhaps you've misjudged him, then," Henri said. "Perhaps we all have. No, we'll let him take the Bernards to Bélesta, and then we can focus all our energies on rescuing Josette."

"But Henri..."

"That's my decision!" Henri snapped before Paul could object. "I'll speak to Max and Julia and tell them exactly what's happening, and that we'll find them a more permanent place of safety as soon as we can."

He hurried away and began talking earnestly to Max and Julia.

"So what do we do?" Paul said to Didier.

"We do as Henri says. He gives the orders; we follow them. And maybe we're worrying too much. Maybe Alain is all right."

"You don't believe that any more than I do," Paul said, glancing over at Alain.

Their eyes met and Alain smiled broadly, nodding

ingratiatingly, and Paul was more certain than ever that he could not be trusted.

Alain moved off with Max and Julia soon after. Before leaving, he shook hands with Henri and promised faithfully to look after his two charges like they were family.

"Family's never meant much to Alain," Eddie said quietly to Paul as they watched them disappear through the trees. "We usually only see him when he wants something."

It didn't make Paul feel any better.

The day had grown warm. The sky was cloudless. Shafts of sunlight pierced the tight branches of the firs, spotlighting tiny areas of the forest floor.

The twins led the remaining members of Henri's little army towards the house, but took a wide, meandering route intended for safety rather than speed. Just as they had said to Julia, it seemed as though they knew every tree in the forest. As they edged forward, keeping a constant watch for the enemy, half-hidden tracks and disguised pathways would suddenly appear to reveal a clear way through what had seemed like dense and impenetrable bramble or thicket.

The forest floor fell away towards the river and the town of Bélesta. Usually the slope was gradual, but occasionally it was steep. Within the slope there were sudden deep gullies that made staying hidden much easier.

"We could get you right up to the front or the back of the house," Gilbert told Henri, "but that might give our friends in there too much of a surprise, and they'll start shooting. How about if we make ourselves known to them about a hundred metres from the front of the house?"

"Yes," Henri agreed, "but not all of us; we must keep them guessing as to our numbers. I'll step out onto the track with a white flag, to show them we want to negotiate."

Paul was still far from convinced that Henri was the right person to do the talking. "I'll go with you," he said quickly.

"I don't think so, Paul."

"But why not?"

"Because you're very young. The leader of a German military unit might not take kindly to being addressed by someone he considers a boy."

Seeing that Paul was about to protest, Henri held up one hand. "You fight like a man, Paul, far better than me. But we must look stronger than we are; like a team of men." He turned to Didier. "Will you come with me?"

"Of course."

"Good. But let me do the talking."

Paul had another point to make before they moved off again. "We must sound strong as well as look strong, Henri."

"Yes, I know that."

"Then … then perhaps it's best that you don't tell them Josette is your daughter. Don't make it too personal."

"He's right," Henri," Didier added. "If you show any emotion it could make you vulnerable. They'll use that against you."

THIRTY-SEVEN

Rudi Werner debated his shot: heart or head? Heart was the safest and a guaranteed kill, but head was the most dramatic – specialist and spectacular – a true sniper's shot.

He was staring down the barrel of his rifle, sights fixed on the head of a little man with a bushy moustache who had stepped onto the track. He was holding up a stick with a piece of white material, probably a handkerchief, tied to it.

They weren't looking to surrender, Werner knew; they wanted to talk. But for the moment he ignored the white flag and thought about the details of his shot options. He was sure of the distance to within a couple of metres. The day was still, so there was no wind to take into consideration, and he knew that on firing, his Karabiner 98k rifle pulled fractionally high and to the right.

He adjusted his aim minutely, lining up the hooded front sight with the V-shaped notch of the rear sight. He rested his index finger on the trigger. The trigger was a shade heavy, not feather-light, as he would have preferred; it needed firm pressure.

Behind the little fellow stood a younger man. At this distance, their features were not totally defined, but Werner was pretty sure he was one of the ones he had encountered earlier. If he took out Bushy Moustache with a headshot, it meant a chest shot for the younger man. He'd be dead before he could even think about making a run for it.

It was a pity neither of the twins nor the loud-mouthed kid had appeared; they were the ones Werner really wanted to line up in his sights.

Werner took a breath and focused his aim on the little man's head.

"Click," he said softly and swung the rifle a little to the right. "Click," he said again.

He exhaled slowly and smiled. Two dead. Perfect kills.

He lifted his head and turned towards the open door. "Sir?" he called. "We have visitors."

Hauptmann Kurt Lau walked from the house unaccompanied and unarmed. Werner had him covered from the first floor window, so he had no need of a weapon.

The German soldier and the French textile factory owner approached each other slowly, stares fixed on the other.

Didier had taken the white flag from Henri and was following a couple of paces behind him. "Stay calm, Henri," he whispered.

Lau stopped walking first. It was a calculated tactical ploy, forcing Henri to take the final steps to their meeting.

The officer looked perfectly calm and relaxed, nodding acknowledgment as Henri came to a standstill. "Monsieur."

"Sir," Henri replied.

Using all his experience, Lau was quick to try to seize the upper hand. "I assume you've approached with the white flag because you wish to surrender?"

Henri gave a slight smile and remained unruffled. "You know that's not the case. You're surrounded by a superior force; there is no escape for you."

Lau's sharp eyes moved slowly around the treeline. "And where exactly is this superior force?"

"They are watching. From all sides. If you wish for a demonstration of our strength, we could perhaps take out the lorry standing at the back of the house. There are plenty more petrol bombs in our arsenal. That would be a pity, of course, because I understand you need the lorry for your departure tonight."

Standing behind Henri, Didier breathed a little easier. Henri was doing well so far – very well – especially as the reality was that they had no further petrol bombs at all.

"I've come to negotiate and to offer you a safe way out," Henri continued.

"I'm listening," Lau said, shortly, realizing that his opening tactic had got him nowhere.

"First of all, I must make it perfectly clear to you that Max Bernard is nowhere near here and that it will be impossible for you to find him now," Henri said, growing in confidence as negotiations went his way.

"Just tell me your terms," Lau said, curtly.

Henri nodded. "Very well. The Noury twins will return to the house. They will collect the landing torches for your escape tonight and they will accompany you to the plateau to set the torches. When you have gone, they will return with the torches; it will be as though you were never here. We will not interfere at all; in fact, we will withdraw completely."

"We can manage without the Noury twins."

"I don't think so. We simply will not let you get near to the torches or the lorry. As I said before, we have plenty more petrol bombs."

Lau considered for what felt like an age to Henri and Didier. "And what is it you require in return for this generous offer?"

For the first time, Henri hesitated, and when he spoke his voice had lost its strength and confidence. "All … all we want," he said haltingly, "is for you to set free my … the prisoner you are holding."

Somehow Henri had made the demand sound like a humble plea, almost as though he was begging, and Lau, a tough negotiator, instantly spotted the weakness.

"She's wounded, you know," he said, "and quite seriously."

Henri sucked in a breath. "Give her back to us," he said quickly, his voice breaking slightly. "I just want you to give us back…"

"Josette?" Lau said softly.

Henri nodded. "Give her back to me. Please?"

Lau waited. The tables had turned. Now, he realized, he was in a position to make some conditions of his own. "She's your daughter."

It wasn't a question, it was a statement of fact, confirmed by Henri's silence.

"These are my terms," Lau continued, much more confidently now. "I'll agree to the Noury twins returning to help us with our departure. I'll agree to all your conditions, but I'll keep Josette with us for now."

"No," Henri gasped.

"She'll come with us to the plateau, as insurance. When we leave, and as long as there have been no further attempts on the safety of my men, Josette will remain behind with the Noury twins."

"Please, please leave her now," Henri said desperately. "You have my word; we'll go. We'll clear the forest now, I promise you. And we won't return. We'll go nowhere near the plateau."

Lau remained unmoved. "This is war, monsieur. Words are given, promises made and then broken."

Didier had struggled to remain silent, but now that Henri had surrendered the initiative to the German officer, he had to speak. "How badly wounded is she?"

Lau nodded. His voice softened; he was not a man without compassion. "It is a serious wound, but I've done my best with it. I'll keep her fluids up during the day, but she needs blood. A transfusion."

"But if you keep her with you, it will be hours before we can get her to a hospital."

The German officer's face hardened again. "I have to think of my own men. One of them is in a worse condition."

The three men stood in silence, Lau unwilling to give ground, Henri desperate not to give up and Didier unsure of what he might say or do next.

As they stood facing one another, the front door of the house opened, and Erich Steidle appeared.

"Sir?" he called to his officer. "Sir?"

Lau glanced back before speaking to Henri again. "Will you wait here?"

Henri nodded and Lau walked quickly back to his second-in-command.

"What is it?"

"It's Wilhelm, sir, he's dead. He swallowed the cyanide."

Lau sighed deeply and his body seemed to sag. "Go on."

"I was with the girl, giving her a drink. She didn't look good and I thought she might pass out. So I wasn't watching Wilhelm when he came round. Berg saw him take out the capsule. He shouted to me, but I wasn't quick enough, Wilhelm already had it in his mouth. He said to tell you he was sorry, then he … then he bit down on it. It was over in seconds, sir."

Lau said nothing, so Steidle continued. "He knew that getting him back to the plane alive would slow us down, and that he probably wouldn't make it. He wanted to make it easier for us, to give us a better chance."

"Yes," Lau said, in little more than a whisper. He turned and walked back to Henri and Didier.

"A change of plan," he said shortly. "I agree to your terms."

Henri's face registered his confusion.

"Josette will be returned to you now. And I'll trust you to keep your word."

"I … I will. But … why?"

"Take your daughter to hospital, monsieur; get her the blood and the treatment she needs."

THIRTY-EIGHT

Josette smiled weakly at her father as she was helped from the house by the German officer. She was pale and drained of her usual fiery energy, and she stumbled slightly as Henri reached out his arms.

Lau held her tightly to prevent her from falling, then stood back as Henri took a firm grip. "Thank you," he mumbled to Lau. He wrapped his arms around his precious daughter and they waited for Didier to return with the car. He had hurried away down the track after a few brief words of explanation to Paul and the twins.

Knowing that a truce had been declared, they slowly emerged from the forest, first Paul, then Gilbert and Eddie. They walked cautiously up to Henri under the watchful eyes of Rudi Werner, still in his sniper's nest but under strict orders not to fire.

The mood remained tense, uncertain; there was no sense of victory, and even when Josette was escorted from the house there was no thought of celebration. Everyone was battered, relieved and grateful to be alive.

Lau glanced around and took in Henri's ragged little army.

"And the rest?" he asked.

Henri simply shrugged his shoulders slightly.

The hint of a smile crossed Lau's face and he nodded. He turned to the twins. "You have nothing to fear. You will be treated respectfully; I trust you will fulfil your side of the bargain."

The twins had not forgotten their earlier treatment, and Gilbert's bruised face bore evidence of the rough handling he'd suffered. But they were loyal to Henri and his group now.

"We'll do as you want," Gilbert said.

"As long as you promise not to offer to pay us," Eddie added.

Lau smiled again, this time wryly. "You have my word."

For the first time in what seemed like days, Paul was thinking of something other than tactics and plans. Glimpsing Inigo lying dead on the forest floor had brought back vivid memories of seeing his own father dead on the ground in Antwerp the previous year, shot in the back as he ran from pursuing German soldiers.

It was an agonizing memory made even worse by the fact that Paul had been unable to help his father in any way. Inigo was beyond help too, now, but there was still something Paul felt he could do for him.

"Our friend is dead in the forest," he said to Lau.

"Will you let the twins bring him in?"

"Of course," Lau replied. "There is also the unfortunate Monsieur Forêt to consider. He's still in his car."

"We'll sort that too," Eddie said. "We'll drive him to Lavelanet tomorrow – maybe even later tonight, when you've gone. We'll leave him somewhere he'll be found."

The sound of an engine signalled Didier's return and they turned to watch him drive up in Henri's car.

Henri and Paul helped Josette into the back seat and then Henri nodded to Paul to join her. He closed the door and turned to the German officer. "Thank you," he said.

"I wish you good luck," Lau said, offering his hand.

"And you also," Henri said as they shook hands.

He climbed into the passenger seat. Didier shoved the car into gear and drove away.

"My bike's still at the end of the track," Didier said to Henri.

"Leave it, we'll come back for it."

Didier nodded. "But we should stop at Bélesta to make sure Max and Julia are safe."

"We must get Josette to hospital."

"Papa, I'm all right," Josette mumbled from the back seat. "I can wait a little longer."

Henri turned to Paul. "And once Josette is in hospital, we'll concentrate on getting you to Puivert tonight. I haven't forgotten *Eagle*."

As the car bumped down the track, Paul took Josette's

hand in his and squeezed it gently. She smiled. They turned and looked back through the rear window.

Lau had not moved. He was watching them go.

THIRTY-NINE

They were not there.

Antoine and Rosalie Granel had seen nothing of Max and Julia Bernard and were certain they had been nowhere near Bélesta that day.

Rosalie Granel, as feisty now as she had been when facing up to five German soldiers, was furious. "You had them both safe and you've lost them again!" she said, eyes blazing. "How could you do that! How could you let them out of your sight?"

Henri was crestfallen. "I thought we could trust him."

"Who?"

"Alain Noury."

"Never heard of him! How could you let anyone drive away with them if you weren't completely certain he could be trusted?"

"I thought he truly wanted to help."

"*Thought!* What use is that! No wonder we're losing the war with people like you in charge!"

Antoine Granel, red-faced and flushed, brushed a strand

of his wispy grey hair from his face. "Rosalie, please! Monsieur Mazet and his friends have done everything they can."

"Yes, and look where it's got us!"

Paul and Didier remained silent, not wanting to make Henri feel any worse than he already did.

They were standing by the front door of the Granels' home. Josette was still in the car, and despite the blow of discovering that the Bernards had been spirited away by Alain Noury, Henri's first concern was still getting his daughter to hospital as quickly as he could.

"You're quite certain they're not in their own house?" he said to Rosalie.

"Go and check if you want," Rosalie said, indignantly, "but I know they're not there. I know everything that happens, or doesn't happen, in Bélesta. I went in after the Germans left and locked it up. No one's been in there since; go and look for yourself if you don't believe me."

"It's not that I don't believe—"

"Go and look," Rosalie ordered, glaring at Henri.

Paul ran over to the house and found both front and back doors locked. He peered in through the windows and saw that the house had remained undisturbed since Rosalie's visit.

"What can he possibly hope to gain by keeping them?" Henri asked when Paul returned.

"I think I know," Paul said. "He heard the twins talking

about the big money they were getting for helping deliver Max to the Germans. The last payment is due tonight, when they leave. That's what he's after: he's going to try to sell the Bernards to the Germans."

"Yes. Yes, that must be it. He's going to take them back to the forest."

"I don't think so. As far as he knows we're still there, or at least some of us are. We said nothing in front of Alain about leaving the forest, so going back in with the Bernards would be too much of a risk."

"So he's waiting on the plateau?"

Paul shook his head. "He'd be too exposed out there in the open, and he'd have to hang around for too long."

"Where, then?"

Paul turned to Didier. "You said he had a house in Espezel."

Didier nodded. "It was his parents' place, where he was brought up. And it's on the plateau. That's where he's taken them."

"Planning to wait for the Germans until after dark," Paul added. "He'll drive out to meet them with the Bernards as his prisoners."

"Then you must go and save them," Rosalie Granel said. "Go now, quickly."

"But I must get my daughter to hospital," Henri said.

Rosalie looked over to the car. "Your daughter? What's wrong with her?"

"She was wounded. She's lost a lot of blood."

Rosalie's face instantly softened. "Why didn't you tell me that in the first place, you silly man!" She bustled off towards Henri's car. "Antoine, go and fetch our car. You can take Monsieur Mazet and his daughter to Lavelanet."

"Yes, Rosalie," Antoine said obediently and hurried away.

"And you boys must go to bring Max and Julia back from Espezel," Rosalie said as Paul, Didier and Henri followed her towards the car.

"We must try," Paul said to Henri. "Everything we've done over the past few days will be for nothing if we don't stop Alain now."

"It's dangerous, I should help you."

"No, Henri," Didier said. "You have to stay with Josette."

"But Alain is armed! I saw the pistol he's carrying."

"And I have my shotgun in the car."

"Do you know the house?" Paul asked Didier.

"Espezel is a small place. Anyone there will tell us where it is."

"But there's still Puivert tonight," Henri said anxiously to Paul. "You must be there by eleven thirty, ready for the plane."

"There's time, Henri, plenty of time."

Rosalie had already opened the back door of the car. Josette was curled up to one side, her face resting on the window, eyes closed.

"The poor child has fainted," Rosalie gasped.

But then Josette opened her eyes. They widened as she saw four anxious faces staring in at her.

"I feel tired, Papa," she said to Henri, "really tired."

"We're leaving for the hospital now," Henri told her. "Antoine is taking us in his car."

As her father and Rosalie helped her from the car, Josette was too weary even to ask why there had been a change of plan.

Paul, ready to leave, took Josette by the hand. "We know where the Bernards are," he said slowly and deliberately. "We're going to get them."

Josette's eyelids flickered; she was only just conscious. "Is it ... is it dangerous?"

"We'll be fine. Didier has his shotgun."

"But you will be careful, both of you."

"We will," Didier said, "and we'll see you later."

"But you're leaving tonight," Josette said turning back to Paul, her eyes suddenly wider. "I *will* see you before you go?"

"Of course," Paul said. "We'll get Max and Julia away from Alain and bring them back to Lavelanet."

"You promise?"

"I promise." He smiled. "I couldn't leave without saying goodbye to you, could I?"

FORTY

Even when the day was at its brightest it felt more like night inside Alain Noury's house at Espezel. Daylight rarely found its way through the shuttered windows into the dusty corners and recesses.

The house stood alone, away from the wide central area of the village, on a narrow road leading uphill towards the bigger town of Belcaire. From a distance it was imposing, and in Alain's grandparents' time it had been an impressive house. But times had changed, the family fortunes had dwindled and now the building had lost its grandeur and was sadly dilapidated.

Roof tiles were cracked or missing, allowing winter snows and hard rains to find their way through to the top floor; one exterior wall bulged at the bottom while another leaned in dangerously at the top; the windows and shutters were mostly bare of paint and riddled with rot. Close up it made a sorry sight.

The interior was even worse: its pervasive dank, musty atmosphere contrasted starkly with the clean, clear mountain air outside.

Thick cobwebs matted the high, paint-flaked ceilings, some of them spiralling downwards in long, tight columns. Wallpaper curled free from the plaster, while rotting floorboards were spongy underfoot or broken completely in places. Mouse and rat droppings littered the floors and even the flat surfaces of some of the furniture.

The house was exactly how Alain liked it.

Alain was a hoarder, a collector. He bought and sold, but his purchases far outnumbered his sales. He would buy almost anything and then find space for it somewhere amid the massive, dark oak furniture that had stood in the same place since being hauled into position by his grandfather.

There were stacks of unmatched, patterned crockery, much of it chipped; black iron cooking pans nesting one inside another; empty glass pickling jars; piles of dusty, moth-ravaged rugs, bed sheets and woollen blankets. Old, crudely painted oils, many faded from the sun, stood against the walls along with smeared and pitted mirrors in broken gilt frames. Sideboard and cupboard drawers could hardly be opened, stuffed as they were with odd pieces of cutlery, boxed sets of fish knives and more fabric; linen, lace, cotton.

Then there was the furniture Alain had added: armchairs with springs poking through the coverings, rickety tables and wonky chairs; most of it was worthless. A massive, glass-fronted bookcase was packed to capacity with dusty, crumbling volumes that Alain had never opened, let alone read. And the tools: hammers, hoes, long-handled scythes, garden spades, shovels and sieves.

The house was a dump and a dumping ground, and Alain was always at his happiest when he was there among his things.

His blue van was parked at the back of the house. It had to be close to the wall, for the space between house and garden, once a wide terrace, had dwindled to virtually nothing as thick weeds relentlessly sprouted and spread.

Beyond the terrace was a garden, now an overgrown jungle, where thick creepers and ivy were gradually strangling the life from the once abundant fruit trees. Alain never ventured into the garden.

He had made coffee and offered it, in chipped cups, to Max and Julia Bernard. They refused and watched in silence while Alain sipped his.

The Bernards were sitting on upright, wooden chairs, hands tied behind their backs to the chairs.

"Can't you untie us?" Julie asked. "This rope is hurting my wrists."

Alain was facing them in a sagging armchair. He smiled shrewdly. "I'm afraid I can't do that. You're very valuable; I can't afford to lose you."

"You could be condemning us to death if you go through with this plan," Max said.

Alain shrugged. "I'm sorry, but it's business. Don't take it personally."

"Let my wife go, then; it's only me they want."

"I'll let our German friends decide that."

"But you don't even know where to meet them or what time they'll get to the plateau."

"Oh, I know exactly where to meet them: I saw my cousins there with them the other day. They told me some ridiculous story about finding land for grazing cattle, but they couldn't fool me: they were checking out the landing site. So we'll get there after dark and then wait. It's quiet, so we won't be disturbed."

There was a sudden movement against one wall as a mouse scurried along the skirting board before disappearing behind a cupboard.

Alain smiled again. "They're quite friendly." The smile faded. "I don't have many friends, you know, not even my cousins, really. They won't be too pleased when I turn up on the plateau with you – I'll be taking the money they were meant to have. But it's their own fault. They should have cut me in from the start."

He picked up a pistol from a small side table jammed against the armchair and studied it. "You know, I've had a difficult time these last months, so it's about time my luck changed."

Max and Julia remained silent and Alain gave them a hostile glare, his eyes flicking from one to the other. "Don't you want to know why?"

"Yes, tell us why," Max said quickly. "We're very interested."

Alain grinned and settled back in the chair. "Well, there was Victor Forêt, of course, though he's not a problem any more. But my real troubles started last summer. It had all been going so well before that." His face darkened. "Then Henri Mazet and his crowd messed everything up. They almost ruined my life."

"Henri?" Max said. "How did Henri do that?"

"Well, if you really want to know, I'll tell you."

He took his time, explaining everything in great detail, revealing how he and his friends, Yvette Bigou and Gaston Rouzard, had teamed up with the Andorrans to rob and murder Jews escaping across the Pyrenees through the Eagle Trail into Spain.

"Making a fortune, we were," he said, "until Henri Mazet and his friends came along. That kid, Paul, was meant to cross into Spain, but they worked out what was going on and killed our Andorran friends. They were onto Yvette. I knew she'd tell them everything, even about me, so I had to kill her. I had no choice. And then Gaston – I couldn't give them the opportunity of speaking to him. He always was a loud mouth. So I shut him up for good."

He held up the pistol and pointed it at Max. "With this."

FORTY-ONE

Peering through a gap in a broken shutter, Paul could just see the glimmer of candlelight reflected in the grimy windowpane.

Moving slowly, he crept along the wall, ready to spring back into cover. He reached the back door and waited, listening, but heard nothing.

Didier was watching from no more than five metres away, hidden in tall grasses and weeds, his shotgun at the ready. He'd told Paul that he would not hesitate to take Alain out if it came to a shooting match. Their lives were at stake. Again.

Paul gripped the metal handle, pushed it down and applied a little pressure to the door. It moved; it was unlocked. Alain was obviously feeling confident – perhaps too confident. Pulling the door shut, Paul carefully released his hold and moved silently back into the cover of the weeds.

"It's not locked," he said quietly to Didier.

"Better than we hoped," Didier replied. "Are you ready, then?"

Paul nodded.

"Knock as loudly as you can; shout as well."

"Oh, he'll hear me, don't worry."

They had decided on another diversionary tactic. The hope was that with Paul hammering at the front door, Alain would go to investigate, giving Didier the chance to burst in through the back door in a surprise attack.

If Alain was unarmed or threw down his gun and surrendered, all well and good, but if he even raised the pistol, Didier would let him have it with both barrels.

"Good luck," Paul whispered as he hurried away.

It was nearly dark. They had known for certain that Alain and his prisoners were in the house as soon as they arrived and spotted the open-backed blue van at the rear of the building. But they chose to wait for the shadows of evening to aid their attack, hoping, too, that the passing hours would increase Alain's confidence and that as a result he might drop his guard.

It seemed, with the unlocked door, that perhaps he had.

Time was ticking and the countdown to *Eagle* had begun, but they knew they would get only one chance with their rescue bid. It seemed better to wait, to plan and prepare, rather than crash straight in as soon as they arrived.

But now they were on the move.

Readying himself to burst in through the back door, Didier edged slowly forward. Once the noise started, he would give it ten seconds – any longer could leave Paul, who was unarmed, in big trouble. He peered through the gap in the shutter and saw the candlelight seem to flicker momentarily as though someone had passed by, causing a draught.

Breathing in deeply, Didier took a couple more steps and then waited.

The noise began: a rapid pounding on the front door and Paul's voice loud and clear in the still evening air.

"Come on, open up!" he bawled. "Open up, Alain, we know you're in there; you can't escape! Give up while you can! Come on, open up!"

Didier completed his countdown, and as the hammering and shouting continued he grabbed the door handle, pushed it down and burst inside.

He found himself in a small kitchen, where a steaming coffee pot perched on top of an ancient cooker.

It was dark, difficult to see. There was another closed door to the right; Didier realized it had to lead to the room where the candle flickered and where, hopefully, Alain and his prisoners were waiting.

There was no time to stop and consider; the shouts and knocking at the front door, muffled now, were continuing. Didier knew he had to keep moving forward. He kicked at the connecting door with the sole of his boot, sending it crashing back on the hinges and smashing into a stack of crockery. Plates and saucers shattered on impact as Didier moved into the adjoining room, shotgun raised.

He stopped.

It was a large room, gloomy, dark and dusty, furniture and clutter everywhere.

On the far side, Max and Julia Bernard sat facing him, side by side on two upright chairs. Their hands appeared to be tied behind their backs and their mouths were gagged. Alain stood immediately behind them, looking surprisingly unconcerned.

"We thought you'd never come in," he said, smiling, "skulking around outside like that for so long. Well, don't just stand there, Didier, come right in, and I'll let your friend in, too. He'll lose his voice if he carries on shouting like that."

Didier didn't move.

"Don't worry, I'm not armed," Alain said. He pointed to a nearby cupboard. "Look, my pistol's on there. You've nothing to worry about, come on in."

"Stand back, then," Didier ordered, his eyes fixed on Alain's as he took a step forward onto a faded red rug covering the floorboards. "And lift your hands up so I can see them."

"All right," Alain said raising his arms obligingly. "I don't know why you're so worried; I can't hurt you from over here. And I really ought to let your friend in."

Didier took another hesitant step forward and then one more, and as he glanced fleetingly at Max Bernard, he saw too late that Max was frantically shaking his head. The rug sank down and the floorboards gave way, and with a snapping and splintering of rotted wood, Didier plunged feet first into the cellar. He yelled once and then crashed heavily onto the hard mud floor.

Then there was silence: even the shouting and hammering at the front door stopped.

"Oh, dear," Alain said brightly. "Didier seems to have fallen. I do hope he's not hurt himself."

FORTY-TWO

Paul heard Didier yell and then a deep rumble, like thunder, from inside the house, and as he looked to his right he spotted a cloud of dust billowing up from a tangle of weeds by the front wall.

He moved across, covering his face. He pushed away the weeds and saw a grille made up of thick iron bars set into the ground. It was obviously an access to a cellar and Paul realized that his friend must have somehow fallen into it.

As the dust cleared, he grabbed two of the bars and heaved. They didn't budge; the grille was set in concrete.

"Didier!" Paul hissed, unable to see into the inky black hole. "Didier, can you hear me?"

There was no reply and no sound from the darkness, but as Paul stared he suddenly heard a key turn in the locked front door.

Paul leapt to his feet; he was a lightning fast runner. He had turned the corner of the house before the door opened and Alain Noury stepped out, pistol in hand.

"Paul," he called warmly. "Paul, come and join us. We're waiting for you. Didier's waiting for you – I think he might have hurt himself. I need your help."

Pressed against the side wall of the house, Paul made an instant decision. He ran to his left, quickly and silently.

Alain looked to his right and then to his left. He sighed. There was no sign of Paul.

It was fortunate for Alain that his property stood on its own, a little away from the rest of the village and prying eyes. People were nosy and Alain liked his privacy.

He took a few steps from the house. On the far side of the narrow road running past the front of the house was a line of trees.

He's probably hidden in there and is staring at me this very moment, Alain thought. He scanned the line of trees, looking for movement. "Paul?" he called again. "Paul, it's no use hiding there, I can see you quite clearly."

Raising the pistol in his right hand, he walked to the edge of the road. He stopped, eyes moving along the trees for a second time. He focused on one tree, took aim, and then suddenly swung around to face the house, eyes darting from one side to another.

"Thought you might try to creep up on me," he breathed. "But maybe you've made a run for it."

He lowered the pistol and walked slowly back to the house, staying alert, looking from one side to the other until he reached the door. He went inside, closed the door and relocked it.

Max and Julia were still in their chairs in the large sitting room, backs to the front window, their heads turned to one side to watch Alain as he came in.

"Can't find him," Alain said to them brightly. "Think he's run for it. Deserting Didier: what sort of a friend is that? Not a very good one, in my opinion."

And then Paul leapt at him.

Using all his weight and force, Paul smashed into his target just below the shoulder, and as they toppled over, the pistol in Alain's right hand spun free, bounced once and disappeared into the hole in the floor.

Paul was staking everything on this shock attack. He'd hurtled round to the back door, rushed inside, given Max and Julia the signal not to give him away and then squeezed himself in at the side of a cupboard.

Being several years older than Paul and stronger too, Alain might have expected to win a fight between the two of them. He screamed in fury, desperately trying to free himself as they rolled across the floor, dangerously close to the broken floorboards and the gaping hole.

But Paul was up for the battle now. Releasing his hold, he swiftly drew back his fist and delivered a sharp, stinging punch into the side of Alain's face, connecting with his cheekbone.

This time, Alain's scream was of pain rather than fury.

He tried to swing his own arm to get in a punch, but Paul dodged it easily, too fast for the heavier man. He landed a second heavy punch, and as they scrambled to their feet, Paul took a glancing blow to the side of the head as Alain lashed out wildly.

It was all or nothing now. Alain charged in to grab his opponent around the waist, but Paul was faster, kneeing the bigger man in the groin.

Alain gasped in shock and agony. Without stopping to think, Paul headbutted him, making bone-crunching contact with the bridge of Alain's nose.

Blood spurted and Alain toppled backwards. He screamed, rolled from his back onto one side, fat tears mingling with the blood streaming down his face.

"Please, that's enough, that's enough," he wailed. "I give up! Please don't hit me again!" He curled into a ball, both hands to his face, and lay there.

Head spinning, Paul was suddenly aware of Max, grunting and fidgeting on the chair, trying to get his attention. His mouth was still gagged. Paul struggled to his feet and staggered across the room to pull the gag free.

"Untie my hands," Max said, gasping for air. "Let me help you."

Paul nodded. He kneeled again to untie the thin cord. It was a simple knot, but his head was reeling and his hands were trembling from the fight. With his vision blurred, he was struggling to focus. He wiped the back of a hand across his eyes and forehead, and saw that it was smeared with blood. An accompanying jolt of pain made him realize that his own head was bleeding and that he must have split the skin when headbutting Alain. He blinked a few times and his vision began to clear.

The knot was almost undone when Max shouted. "Paul! Paul, he's running!"

Alain was heading for the back door. Paul was still unsteady from the fight. He hauled himself to his feet as the van's engine coughed into life.

"He's getting away," Max said, wriggling to free his hands. "He'll go for the Germans."

"I'll stop him! Paul yelled, sprinting towards the front door.

Alain had left the key in the lock. Paul wrenched open the door and was outside as the van negotiated the tight turn from the back garden. The space was narrow and Alain was driving recklessly, desperate to get away. There was a high-pitched screech as the side of the vehicle scraped against the corner of the wall as it completed the turn.

His head still spinning, Paul stood his ground for a moment, but even in his dazed state he knew that to remain in front of the vehicle would be suicidal. There was only one other option.

He stepped back, and as the van went by, he leapt onto the open back and clung on.

FORTY-THREE

Night had fallen, and in the cloudless spring sky the stars were already piercing the darkness.

Alain had not paused to switch on the van's lights as he jumped into the vehicle and drove off. Now, moving away from the house, it was picking up speed, racing downhill into the village of Espezel.

Paul's hands were wrapped around the metal bar at the top of the backboard behind the driver's cab. He was hanging on for his life.

The wood-planked open back was rough and uneven, with jagged splinters sticking up everywhere. The van was not designed for comfortable travel. It was a working vehicle, used mainly for transporting the many and various items Alain bought or bartered for on his travels. It now sped into the wide, sprawling area that opened like a funnel at the centre of the village. An elderly couple, walking arm-in-arm, stopped and stared as the vehicle, still showing no lights, went tearing by, smoke belching from the exhaust.

Alain knew perfectly well that Paul was clinging

precariously to the backboard; he'd glimpsed his leap and felt the impact as Paul landed heavily on the wooden planks. He glanced back through the small oblong window behind his head and grinned at the young man staring at him through the glass.

Alain's face was a bloody mess and his nose had swollen to twice its normal size, but he seemed oblivious of the pain as he laughed aloud. "Come for a ride, have you, Paul?" he yelled. "Well, I hope you enjoy it!"

Throwing up clouds of dust, the van cleared the village and the driver at last switched on the headlamps. They barely disturbed the darkness of the road ahead.

Paul was on his knees, keeping low, trying to think of how he would or even could halt Alain's flight. But as the van bounced onward and he was tossed from one side to the other, all Paul could focus on was his own survival. At least the rushing night air had cleared his head.

Hardly slowing the vehicle, Alain wrenched at the steering wheel, turning off the main road, which ran in one direction towards the mountain town of Ax-les-Thermes and the Pyrenees and the towns of Quillan and Limoux in the other. He was once again on the small road that cut all the way across the plateau and down through the forest to Bélesta.

He pressed the throttle to the floor, looked over his shoulder to the small window and shouted, "Here we go, then! Hold on tight!" He yanked the steering wheel sharply to the right. Paul's body jerked to the side and he clung on desperately as his legs slithered across the rough wooden planks and his feet dangled over the side edge.

Before he could even haul himself back to the centre, Alain had pulled the wheel the opposite way and Paul was slithering again. This time a needle-sharp splinter pierced his trousers and speared into his leg. He yelled out as the van swerved to the right again and his body slid painfully across the rough wood. One hand lost its grip, and for a few terrifying seconds Paul thought he was going to be thrown off the van to the ground, but with a desperate lunge he managed to grab hold again.

Both his legs were dangling over the edge as Alain hauled the vehicle into another dramatic swerve. But this time Paul pulled in his legs, tucking them tightly against his body so that the sideways movement was much less severe.

Alain looked back and saw Paul's hands clenching the bar.

"Still there, Paul?" he shrieked. "Well, enough is enough. I've got things to do, people to see, so this time it's goodbye."

He wrenched at the steering wheel even harder, and the vehicle swerved so violently that it rose up on two wheels and almost toppled over. Realizing that the manoeuvre had been too extreme, Alain yanked the wheel in the other direction. The van thudded down, swerving wildly, wheels juddering and tyres screaming in protest as the panicking driver wrestled with the wheel, struggling to keep control.

In a last frantic effort, Alain stood on the brakes and the van jerked and bucked like a wild horse. The brakes locked up, and as the vehicle skidded sideways, a threadbare front tyre exploded, sending strips of rubber into the air.

The vehicle's nose dipped to the right, the exposed metal rim of the front wheel sending up a shower of sparks as it made contact with the ground and then dug into the cracked mud at the roadside.

This time the van did go over, crashing down on its side and skidding onward in a cloud of dust and mud.

Paul was flung into the air. All that saved him from death was the fact that the battered vehicle had been slowing dramatically as it went over. He landed on one shoulder and rolled over and over, ending up on his back. The soft, crumbling surface of the plateau had cushioned the impact.

Paul lay still, staring up at the stars, amazed that he was alive and conscious. Slowly he sat up. The van was on its side. The engine had stalled and the lights were smashed. There was no movement. Paul was certain that Alain could not have survived the crash.

But then the door at what was now the top of the vehicle creaked open a little. It fell back, then opened again and fell shut a second time. Alain was trying to get out, but could not push the door fully open.

As Paul got to his feet, he heard the window slide down and then, in the darkness, he saw Alain's head appear. He glanced around before pulling himself up and out onto the side of the vehicle. It wobbled unsteadily and he jumped down to the ground.

Paul was painfully aware of the splinter buried in his leg and what seemed like a hundred bruises on every part of his body, but he remained determined to prevent Alain from getting away. He moved cautiously forward. Alain saw him coming. "Get away from me!" he shouted. "Haven't you had enough?"

Paul said nothing; he just kept walking.

"Get away!" Alain yelled again, then turned and ran onto the plateau.

"Alain!" Paul shouted. "Stop! Give up; it's over! It's madness to run out there; stop!"

But Alain kept running and quickly disappeared into the night.

Paul followed, peering into the darkness, trying to catch sight of Alain and staying alert for lurking danger. The treacherous plateau was risky enough in full daylight, but in darkness it was as dangerous as walking into a minefield.

"Alain!" Paul yelled. "Alain, come back, please!"

There was a sudden short scream and then a splash.

Paul stopped, his eyes wide. "Alain! Alain!"

There was no reply.

"Alain!"

Nothing.

Paul walked on, trying to figure out where the shout had

come from, but on the vast emptiness of the plateau it was almost impossible to judge.

He stumbled forward, repeatedly calling Alain's name and stopping every thirty seconds or so to listen for a sound or a cry for help, but nothing came back.

Treading cautiously he arrived at a hole, no more than a metre and a half across. Standing on the crumbling edge, he stared down and saw water about a metre below, a jet-black pool; a sinkhole. The water appeared undisturbed, and terrifyingly dark. A single bright star up in the night sky was reflected on the surface.

Paul looked up and gazed out in every direction. There was nothing to be seen; the night was perfectly still.

He glanced briefly at the water again and then turned to retrace his steps. The van was no longer in sight.

Paul could see nothing he recognized. He was totally confused and lost.

FORTY-FOUR

There was an overwhelming smell of rotting and fermenting fruit.

Didier had been stunned by the fall into the cellar, but the thick old rug had prevented any broken bones. He came round, feeling as though he had a hangover.

Max and Julia were calling to him.

"Didier!"

Dust was clogging his throat.

"Didier!"

He coughed. "I'm all right," he finally croaked.

"Are you hurt?"

"I … I don't think so."

It was blacker than night in the cellar and looking up, Didier could only just make out the outline of the two heads staring down from above.

"Can you get me out?" he asked, getting to his feet.

"We don't know," Max answered. "It's so dark and there are no electric lights, we can't even find any more candles. There must be some, but in all this clutter…"

"Keep looking," Didier told him as his night vision started to kick in.

He began to explore the cellar, searching for a way out. The entire space appeared to be packed and stacked with food. Cans were piled high on shelves, sacks of vegetables sat against the walls, there were rows of bottles containing preserved and pickled foods, and lines of open trays of apples and pears, piled five or six high.

The cellar was a vast larder.

Didier knew that after the shortages and rationing of the First World War, many older French people had begun to hoard food in case another war came along.

And it had.

He'd never met Alain's parents, but knew they'd been relatively old when their only son was born.

They'd both died years before the Second World War started, and it looked as though their food hoard had remained undisturbed since then, although, as Didier heard scrabbling and squeaking in one corner, he realized that rats and mice were taking a share of what was on offer.

He moved cautiously along one wall and bumped his head against a long, dry bone hanging from a rope. A few shreds of shrivelled meat clung to the bone; Didier realized that this was all that remained of a cured ham.

Moving on, he almost stumbled as one foot encountered the bottom step of a stone staircase set into the side of the wall. He climbed it and came to a heavy old door. He flicked the latch and pushed, but the door was locked.

"Over here!" Didier yelled. "There's a door. See if you can find the key."

He listened as two sets of footsteps crossed the floor above.

"We're here!" Max called from the other side of the door. "Julia found some candles so we can see, but there's no key in the lock."

"Look around," Didier told him. "It has to be somewhere."

Even as he spoke Didier knew that there was no certainty at all that the key was nearby. It could be anywhere: in the house, in Alain's pocket or lost.

He heard Max and Julia rummaging around the room and feared they might well search all night and still not find the elusive key.

Then a thought struck him. "Is there a ceiling beam near the door?" he shouted.

Max's voice came back. "Yes, just above, a big heavy beam."

"Check at the end, near the wall."

After a few seconds Max shouted excitedly. "You're right, there's a key hanging on a nail in the wood!"

Didier heard the key pushed into the lock. It turned.

The door swung open and Didier was face to face with his rescuers.

"How did you know?" Julia asked.

Didier smiled. "My dad always kept the key to our cellar hanging above the door."

Paul had lost track of time.

By starlight, at the sinkhole, he'd tried to check his watch and found the glass smashed and the hands stopped at precisely 9.25. But he had no idea at what point during his battle with Alain the watch had stopped.

Since then he seemed to have been walking for a long time; it took an age just find the road. When he finally did, he turned in the direction of Espezel, and after a further ten minutes or more came upon the blue van.

For a few fleeting moments he thought he might find Alain hiding in the wreckage. He stopped and circled the vehicle warily, his feet crunching over fragments of glass from the shattered windscreen and headlights. Fuel had leaked from the ruptured tank and Paul realized how lucky they had been that the vehicle had not erupted in a ball of flame when it went over. There was no sign of Alain; his luck had not lasted for very much longer.

Paul walked on; no one passed him on the road. He was incredibly weary, his body ached and he was desperate for sleep. The previous night he'd done no more than doze fitfully. Now last night seemed a lifetime ago.

He knew he had to stay alert. He thought about Josette and Didier and then his thoughts drifted to the operation to take him from France that night, the operation codenamed *Eagle*.

In his confused and exhausted state he wondered if perhaps the Lysander plane due to pick him up had already come and gone from Puivert. But surely it couldn't be that late – could it? Whatever the time, Paul knew without doubt that there would be no chance now of returning to Lavelanet to say his farewells to Josette. He would have to break his promise.

He felt in his inside jacket pocket for the letter he'd written the previous evening. Thankfully it was still there. He kept walking, his mind and body aching, his leg throbbing with a nagging pain from the buried splinter.

Reaching the junction with the main road, he stopped and rested for a moment. As he turned towards Espezel he saw, to his joy, the headlights of an approaching car.

It was Henri's car, with Didier at the wheel. And as it slowed to stop, Paul saw Max and Julia in the back seat.

Didier jumped from the car, the engine still running. "Are you all right?"

Almost too weary to answer, Paul nodded.

"And Alain?"

"Out there somewhere," Paul said, pointing back towards the plateau. "He crashed the van and ran off. I tried to stop him but … I think he drowned in one of the pools."

There was no time to stand and talk.

"Get in the car, Paul, we have to get you to Puivert."

Paul pulled open the passenger door and sank into the seat as Didier got behind the wheel.

"The van went over on its side," Paul said. "You'll see it as we cross the plateau."

"We can't go that way."

"Why not?"

"Because at some time tonight – could be any time now – the Germans will be on the plateau to meet their own plane. We can't risk running into them with Max and Julia in the car."

"So where do we go?"

"We take the back route," Didier said, pulling away. "Then cross the plateau on the far side and go down into Puivert. It'll be tight, but if we're fast we might just make it."

FORTY-FIVE

The road was long and winding, much slower than the route across the plateau, especially in darkness. The descent was steep at times, with plunging drops into deep valleys on either side as the road twisted and turned.

Didier was as tired as Paul and was using all his powers of concentration to stay awake and focus on the driving. But more than once he found his eyes closing.

"Tell us what happened with Alain," he said to Max and Julia, blinking and rubbing his eyes after almost swerving off the road on a hairpin bend. "Just keep talking."

Julia went first, explaining how Alain had drawn the pistol as they left the forest track and then driven them at gunpoint to the house in Espezel.

Then Max told the shocked Paul and Didier how their captor had admitted his involvement with the murderous gang that had robbed and slaughtered escapees in the Pyrenees the previous year.

"Alain," Didier said, fully awake now. "I can't believe it!"

"Believe it," Max continued, "because he also told us that when you and Henri got close to discovering exactly what was going, he killed two other people in the gang to stop them from talking."

"Yvette and Gaston? *He* killed them?"

"Yes," Julia said, "Yvette and Gaston, those were the names."

"Alain!" Paul said, shaking his head. "We never considered him, not even in the past couple of days."

"I always thought he was all bluff," Didier added. He glanced in the rear view mirror at Max and Julia. "And we'd never have known if he hadn't told you."

"And he wasn't finished," Max said. "He was still planning to have his revenge on all of you."

Paul shook his head. "He almost started with me tonight."

They fell silent, lost in their own thoughts as the road twisted on.

"What time is it?" Paul asked.

Didier glanced quickly at his watch. "Nearly eleven thirty, they'll be waiting for us by now."

"Are we close?"

"Getting there."

Paul gazed out at the night sky. "I won't get to see Josette after all," he said quietly to Didier.

"I know."

"I promised I'd go back to say goodbye, I wanted to. She'll know I wanted to."

"Of course."

"But you'll explain everything, won't you?"

"Yes, and I'll ... I'll give your goodbyes."

Paul sighed. "And what about Max and Julia? Where will they go?"

Didier shrugged his shoulders. "Henri will work something out."

They were descending quickly now, and as they passed the turning for the tiny village of L'Escale they rounded a long, sweeping bend and glimpsed the dark mass of Puivert Castle, resting serenely on its hilltop site and silhouetted against the night sky.

"We'll make it now – let's hope they're waiting."

Didier drove down into the village of Puivert and continued on through the winding main street.

"Do you know where the landing strip is?" Paul asked.

Didier nodded. "We're almost there."

Just outside the village, he turned the vehicle onto a mud track. There were trees on either side, and beyond the trees the landscape opened into a wide valley.

Didier turned off the headlights and continued down the track on sidelights. They reached what looked like a large shed. It was in darkness, but standing nearby they could just see the outline of two or three stationary vehicles.

Bringing the car to a standstill, Didier switched off the engine and they waited. A minute passed, two minutes, and then figures approached from the shadows.

Didier and Paul began to open the doors.

"Stay exactly where you are!" a voice ordered.

"We've come for *Eagle*," Didier said without moving.

"Where's Reynard?"

"He's … he's with his daughter. She was hurt in another operation."

There was a brief whispered conversation among the shadowy figures.

"Where's the passenger?" the same voice asked.

"Here. Next to me."

"And the others, in the back?"

"They were the other operation," Didier said. "We had to bring them."

A few more brief words were exchanged outside.

"All right. Get out please, all of you."

They climbed from the car and saw immediately that the person they had been conversing with was holding a sub-machinegun. "A present from our German friends," he said as he saw Paul looking.

There were ten more men, some of them armed. They were all similarly dressed in belted jackets; dark, rough cotton shirts; serge trousers and heavy boots.

Paul found himself thinking that it looked like the beginning of some sort of uniform and was thrilled to realize that just as Henri had said, the Resistance movement was at last starting to take serious shape in southern France.

Didier went to speak. "I'm Di—"

"No introductions," said the man who was obviously the leader of the group quickly. "We don't need to know."

Didier nodded. "Of course."

Suddenly, the distant drone of an aircraft could be heard in the still night air, and instinctively they all looked upwards.

"He's coming," Didier whispered to Paul. "This is it."

"Right on time," the Resistance leader said. He turned to the other men. "Positions, everyone."

The shadowy figures hurried away while the leader remained with Paul and the others.

"This has to be quick," he said, "so be ready to run. He'll be landing this way and coming towards us. As soon as he starts to turn, run for the plane; he won't wait around. He'll make the pick-up, taxi back and take off in the same direction as he landed."

The plane was already turning for its landing approach.

"And there'll be no time for long goodbyes," the Resistance leader continued, "so you'd better say what you want to say while you can. I need to join my men. Remember, as soon as he stops, you start running."

He moved quickly away into the field. Paul, Didier, Max and Julia waited.

Paul looked at Didier. "I don't know what to say."

"No, me neither."

"But…"

"Yes?"

Paul shook his head. He reached for the letter in his pocket and took it out.

The drone of the single engine grew louder as the Lysander descended, and suddenly ten strong beams, five on either side, illuminated the grass landing strip.

They caught their first glimpse of the plane as it sank from the sky and passed to its right the ancient walls and turrets of Puivert Castle. The descent looked smooth and steady in the still night air. The Lysander touched down and came bouncing along the landing strip, moving quickly towards them until it came to a brief halt before starting to turn.

And then they were running, racing across the field towards the tiny plane.

Within two minutes the aircraft was climbing back into the sky, leaving Puivert, leaving France, heading first for Spain and then for Portugal.

On the ground, those who remained stood and watched until the plane had disappeared from view and the sound of its engine had faded to silence.

FORTY-SIX
Day Five

Josette sat up in her hospital bed, a plasma drip in her arm. She looked pale and tired, but much better than she had a few hours earlier.

It was one-thirty in the morning, but Josette had refused to even attempt to sleep. She was in a single-bedded room, with her father seated on one side of the bed and her mother on the other.

"What time is it now?" Josette said to Henri irritably.

He sighed. "Ten minutes since you asked me last, Josette."

"But what time is it?"

Henri looked at his watch. "It's one thirty-two."

"He's not coming, is he?"

"Josette, if everything went to plan, by now he'll be over Spain. Perhaps they've even landed to refuel."

"But he promised he'd come."

"Something must have happened; Paul would never deliberately break his promise. We can only hope that they're safe. All of them."

"Josette, will you please try to sleep for a little while?" Hélène added. "You're very weak. The doctor said you needed rest."

"I'm not weak. I've never been weak."

The mood was tense; they were all as anxious as each other.

"Maybe you should go home, Mama," Josette said. "Perhaps Didier has gone there and is waiting for us."

Hélène ignored the comment, knowing perfectly well that Didier would come straight to the hospital when and if he could.

They lapsed into an uneasy silence. Josette was just about to ask her father the time yet again, when suddenly they heard footsteps approaching down the long corridor.

Josette looked at Henri.

"It's the nurse," Henri said, "come to check on you again."

Josette shook her head. "It's not the nurse. She walks faster than that."

The footsteps came closer. Henri slowly stood up and then Hélène got to her feet too. They all stared at the closed door.

There was a gentle tap.

"Come in!" Josette almost shouted.

The door opened and Didier appeared. He was smiling.

"Oh, Didier," Josette breathed, "you're safe."

Henri clasped his hands together and Hélène crossed

herself, looked to the heavens and whispered a few words of thanks.

"Yes, I'm safe," Didier said, grinning.

"And Paul?" Josette said anxiously. "He'd promised he'd come. Is he all right?"

Didier shrugged his shoulders and Josette and her parents exchanged anxious glances.

"What do you mean, Didier?" Josette demanded. "Is he all right or not?"

Didier smiled again. "You'd better ask him yourself."

He stood to one side and Paul walked into the room.

"Paul!" Josette screamed. "I knew you'd come, I knew it!"

"Paul," Henri gasped. "How…?"

Hélène crossed herself again and muttered even more.

"But the plane," Henri said. "Did it not arrive?"

"Oh, yes, it arrived," Paul said, smiling. "The Bernards are on the plane. It won't be a comfortable flight, but there was just about room for two passengers. I hope they like England."

"The pilot was a bit confused," Didier added. "He thought he was taking one passenger to Portugal, but we convinced him that Max and Julia were far more important to the British than Paul would ever be."

"I think he just wanted to get back up into the air as quickly as he could," Paul said, laughing.

"But your father's plans," Henri said, "and everything you have to tell the British…?"

"I wrote it all down in a letter, everything I know. There's nothing more I can tell them. I gave the letter to Julia just before they got on the plane, so the British don't need me now."

"But we do, Paul," Josette said, her eyes shining. "Is that why you changed your mind?"

"I knew last night, really," Paul answered with a shrug. "That's why I wrote the letter. I knew I didn't want to leave" – he hesitated, blushing slightly – "I didn't want to leave any of you."

He sat on the bed close to Josette, then turned to Henri. "And besides, we saw the start of the real Resistance movement in Puivert tonight. There'll be a lot for us to do in the next few months."

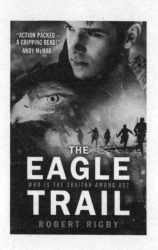